Also by Robin Edwards

For young adults

Slaves!
Enemies!
My Ghost & Me

For adults
Nearly Swinging
The Gravecloth of Christ
Red Incubus
9th of Ramadan

Dodger in Oz

by

Robin Edwards

Dodger in Oz

MoonRiver Books

First Published in 2011
This edition publish 2018

Copyright Robin Edwards 2011

Robin Edwards has asserted his right to be identified as the author of this work in accordance with the Copyright, Design and Patents Act 1988

All rights reserved. No part of his publication may be reproduced, stored in a retrieval system, transmitted in any form or by any means, electronic, mechanical or otherwise, without the express permission of the rights owner.

This book is a work of fiction. Names, characters, places and incidents are used fictitiously and any resemblance to actual persons living or dead is entirely coincidental.

Dodger in Oz

MoonRiver Books

Oliver Twist - by - Charles Dickens

When workhouse orphan Oliver Twist ran away to London, he was found homeless and hungry by Jack Dawkins, the Artful Dodger, who offered him lodgings with a *respectable old man*. Eager to accept, innocent Oliver did not realise that Dodger was a pickpocket who had trapped him into a den of thieves run by a criminal called Fagin.

Oliver's first expedition as an apprentice thief went badly when Dodger and another of Fagin's boys, Charley Bates, were spotted picking an old gentleman's pocket. They ran, as did Oliver who had only been watching. Dodger and Charley escaped, but Oliver was a caught and taken before a magistrate. When a witness testified that another boy had committed the crime, Oliver was taken home by the old gentleman, Mr Brownlow, who felt sorry for him.

Afraid that Oliver might tell the police about his activities, Fagin arranged for Bill Sikes, his girlfriend Nancy and Dodger to kidnap him as he was running an errand to a bookshop for Mr Brownlow. Back in Fagin's clutches, Oliver was forced to help Sikes with burglaries.

Things began to go wrong when Dodger was arrested for stealing, and Oliver was shot whilst burgling a house with Sikes. The police arrested Fagin, but Sikes got away and, discovering that Nancy had tried to reunite Oliver with Mr Brownlow, murdered her. Cornered by the police as he was escaping over the rooftops, Sikes was accidentally killed.

Oliver was reunited with Mr Brownlow who turned out to be his grandfather.

At their trials, Fagin was sentenced to death and Dodger to transportation to Australia.

What follows, is Dodger's story in his own words…

Chapter 1: Trial and Sentence

To this day, I haven't a clue where Mr Charles Dickens got his information, but it certainly wasn't from me, and it couldn't have been from Fagin who was dead, hanged on Newgate gallows years before he had even begun writing *Oliver Twist*. Nancy, that angel of a girl, was dead too, killed by Bill Sikes, who died escaping from the Peelers[1] who had trapped him on a rooftop.

It didn't leave many who knew the proper facts, save for Oliver Twist himself, who's now a bigwig lawyer in America, and Mr Brownlow his Grandpa.

You couldn't make it up, as they say, and Mr Dickens didn't, well, not all of it. He was a court reporter in those days and could have been at Fagin's trial, and he does tell how Oliver and Mr Brownlow visited Fagin in his cell the night before he was hanged.

---

[1] Policemen, named after the founder of the police force, Robert Peel.

At the time, I hadn't a clue that Mr Brownlow and Oliver were related but, supposing I had, things might have turned out very different. I mean, after Nancy, Bill and me kidnapped him while he was returning Mr Brownlow's books, and dragged him back to Fagin's place, I might have chanced my luck and helped him escape, or tipped off Mr Brownlow as to where he was hidden. The old gent would have coughed up money in a trice and, you never know, might even have taken pity on yours truly and adopted me as well as Oliver. To think, we could have been brothers.

The truth is, when I saw Oliver bathed, dressed posh clothes and acting as polite as a Sunday school teacher, I was downright jealous.. What was so special about him? Why should he have been given a decent life, a family, money and an education? Why not me or Nancy, or my best mate Charley Bates? Any of us would have jumped at the chance of a feather bed in a warm house with grub on the table three times a day.

No, jealousy got the better of me though, I confess, I did feel a twinge of guilt, which was unusual. Afterall, when you're a thief by trade you can't go pinching other folks' belongings and have a conscience. So, I chose the devil I knew best, Fagin. At least with him I had a regular place to sleep if rat-infested, and food in my belly if maggoty, which was a sight more than those with empty stomachs and only the gutter to sleep in. Such luxury came with a daily clip round the ear or a kick in the backside when the swag wasn't to Fagin's liking.

I only found out the whole story because Alfie Watchit, the famous Lambeth forger, taught me reading while we were being transported to Australia on a prison ship. You could have knocked me down with a feather, when I saw the title, *Oliver Twist,* in gold letters on the cover of a book in a library there. I've kept it to this day and it's still a miracle to me how Mr D pieced the story together. Not that he's always correct, and he takes liberties with his descriptions of yours truly, though not as many as Mr George Cruickshank, the so-called artist, whose sketches leave much to be desired. Fagin is probably turning in his grave at being drawn with that great hooked nose, and he pictures me as a midget with a face that's a cross between a monkey and a butcher's dog. It just proves neither of 'em ever met me because, as many would testify, I was a handsome cove in those days and a dapper dresser too.

To be fair, since then I've read all Mr D's books and I must admit he has quite a knack for story telling. So much so, that everything he wrote was snapped up as soon as it arrived in Australia on boats from England, even if it had taken six months to get there.

I knew Fagin had met a bad end because I had seen his body on the gallows as us convicts were being marched to Deptford to await the ship that would take us to the other side of the world. It was his coat I recognised first, bottle green with huge pockets that held plenty of loot, billowing like a sail, turning him in the breeze. I stared and our eyes met, though he couldn't see me, him being dead and all. Is he in Heaven or is he in Hell? I'd still like to know, because sure as eggs are eggs I'll end up in the same place.

I was taking it in that dreadful sight, when a gaoler whacked me across the knees with a truncheon and bawled at me to get a move on. They were no angels those brutes and would crack your skull as soon as spit on the cobbles.

I can't remember anything before Fagin who, so say, found me on his doorstep. He, Charley Bates, Fagin's other boys and Nancy were the only family I ever knew. My nifty fingers soon made me his top chap and I earned that old devil a fortune dodging ladies and gents for their purses and the silk handkerchiefs that made good prices once the owners' initials had been unpicked with a pin. In return, I got sausages and a cup of gin for supper and the occasional coin for myself when he was feeling generous or wanted to shut me up because Bill Sikes was asking difficult questions.

Ignorance don't make anything right. A thief's a thief whichever way you look at it, and must swallow his medicine when it falls due. When the law collared me, I was banged to rights because the snuffbox I'd nicked was still in my pocket. It wasn't even silver, just cheap tin-plate worn through to the brass. It wouldn't have fetched a ha'penny and Fagin would have booted my backside for even daring to bring it back, but it was evidence of my guilt, on top of which the law had witnesses to swear they'd seen me picking the gent's pocket.

Mr D describes what happened in court almost as if he had watched the proceedings himself, as he might well have done. Admittedly, I did swagger in protesting about the disgraceful position an honest chap like me had been put in.

'Hold your tongue!' the gaoler warned.

'I am an Englishman, ain't I?' I replied in a voice those at the back of the court could hear. 'Where are my privileges?'

'You'll get them soon enough,' he said, 'and salt and pepper with 'em.'

I was not to be beaten by the likes of him.

'We'll see what the Secretary of State for Home Affairs has to say about that,' I said, 'and I thank the magistrates not to keep me waiting, for I have an appointment in the City. I am a punctual man and if I miss it I may bring an action for damages!' I always was a cheeky blighter and the crowd roared at my antics.

'Silence!' cried the gaoler.

'And what do we have here?' asked the magistrate setting aside his quill.

'A case of pick-pocketing, sir,' said the clerk.

'Has he been here before?'

'He ought to have been,' said the gaoler. 'I know him as a thieving scoundrel.'

'Oh, so you know me, do you?' I said, all sarcastic. 'Well, that's defamation of character if ever I heard it and I shall be taking action for damages against you.'

The crowd was convulsed with laughter at my clowning.

'Where are the witnesses?' asked the clerk.

The Peeler who'd arrested me gave evidence, calling me an out-and-out vagabond, then a couple of upright citizens identified me as the culprit, to which I replied that once my lawyer arrived they'd wishing they'd told the truth and treated me better.

It did no good. In fact, if I hadn't cheeked the gaoler, Peeler, witnesses, clerk and magistrate, I might have got off lighter but, such was my character, that I gave them plenty of lip and enjoyed the laughs as I puffed out my chest like I was Prime Minister Lamb riding to Parliament.

'How old are you?' The magistrate peered over his spectacles.

Still acting the big man, I replied, 'Fifteen, your honour.' I wasn't of course, twelve being more like it, but the clerk dutifully wrote fifteen in his ledger and that was what cooked my goose.

The magistrate shook his head. 'Rather small for his age, isn't he? Not getting enough meat, I imagine. Have you questioned him about his accomplices, officer?'

'He will not give the names of the gang, sir,' said the Peeler, who would have liked to beat them out of me with his truncheon.

'I'm no nark!' I shouted to cheers. 'You'll get nothing from me.'

'Very well, so be it,' said the magistrate wearily and, with that, sentenced me to transportation..

Transportation. I'd heard of it, and knew of a felon or two who'd drawn the same straw, though I had no idea what being shipped to Australia really meant. I'd heard Sikes saying that the weather was better, no rain or horrible yellow fogs off the Thames. It was warm in summer and warm in winter, and instead of passing time locked in a stinking cell with twenty others, criminals worked on farms in the open air, ate fresh food and drank lovely white milk instead of beer and gin. It all sounded like the holidays rich folk took, and a sight better than doing time in Newgate.[2]

Little did I know that if I'd told the truth about my age the case would have gone another way since they had stopped transporting children years before.

When the magistrate banged his gavel and told the gaoler to take me down, the crowd cheered me like a hero all the way to the cells in the yard where they locked you up until you went to prison. They liked to see someone cocking-a-snook at authority, but as soon as the door slammed and I was out of

---

[2] A London prison, originally the gatehouse to the city's west gate, rebuilt and enlarged with money left by London's most famous mayor, Dick Whittington. It was demolished in 1902 to make way for the new Central Criminal Court, better known as the Old Bailey,

sight, they forgot me and turned to the next unlucky soul waiting in the dock.

I remember it as if it was yesterday.

I sobbed and cried for my mother, not that I remembered her, and beat the door for them to let me out until there wasn't a tear left in me, and my fists were raw and bleeding from hammering on solid oak. The gaolers had seen and heard plenty of tough lads going girly before, and taunted me by saying that if I didn't hush my noise they'd throw in rats to gnaw my legs off.

It was a dark Friday night and the crowds had dispersed by the time they chained me to three others, herded us into a cart and hauled us through the streets to Newgate Prison. Fagin was already there, in the condemned cell, waiting to be hanged. Not that I knew it until Monday morning when I witnessed his bulging eyes and lolling tongue as he swung on the scaffold.

In his book, Mr Dickens tied up most of the loose ends, but he never said what happened to me after my trial, if you can call it a trial. I was guilty, no question. Not that it would have made a jot of difference if I'd been as innocent as a newborn lamb. The magistrate had made up his mind that he was sending me *down under,* as they called Australia, before he'd even set his beady eyes on me. *Transportation for seven years* was the sentence the clerk wrote in his ledger.

I admit I had it coming, but I was only twelve and a thief since I could remember. Not that such employment was my choice, but I had no say in the matter. I would have preferred to have been a lawyer, banker or Member of Parliament, thieves the lot of them but legal if you take my meaning. Anyhow, I hadn't been to Eton College or Cambridge University, so I didn't have the right connections. However, I did have one talent. I was a natural at what Fagin called *dodging*, which is how I came by my monniker[3], Artful Dodger.

John Dawkins is my real name, Jack for short, and that's what they call me to this day.

---

[3] Nickname

Chapter 2: Newgate Prison

Mr Dickens has a lot to say about prison in his books. I've read them all and, take it from me, he's not exaggerating one bit. He had some experience, because after his family moved from Portsmouth to Camden Town in London, his dad was locked up in Marshalsea Prison for debt. By all accounts, he owed a packet, but never went as far as putting his children on the streets to pick pockets. As chance would have it, young Charles turned out to be one of the lucky ones, and it wasn't long before his dad came into an inheritance and he was packed off to Wellington House Academy like one of the posh heroes in his books; Copperfield, Twist and Pip. I'm not being fair on the man. When he was twelve, he was slaving thirteen hours a day in a Wapping bootblack factory for miserable wages, so he knew something about the plight of the working class. Credit where credit's due, he pulled himself up by the bootstraps and made something of himself. I, on the other hand, at the same age, was a convicted thief on my way to Australia in chains for seven years.

I can't remember much about the three nights I spent in Newgate, but being banged up in that hellhole was enough to terrify the breeches off Satan himself. Dealing with Fagin and Sikes was one thing, being surrounded by lags who'd do murder for a farthing[4] was another and you had to keep your wits about you. So, while I was fighting them off from stealing the silver sixpences sewn into the lining of my coat for emergencies, it didn't leave much time for taking in the finer points of my surroundings. I laid low, sneaked into a corner, huddled down in the straw, and closed my ears to the screams and moans and tried to think of better times. Not that there had ever been many of those, which set me off blubbing like a baby and feeling sorry for myself at the thought of what lay ahead.

Cold and hungry, I cried myself to sleep.

Saturday and Sunday were no better. There was rowdiness, fighting and drunkenness. If you had money, cheap gin was available by the gallon from the gaolers, but I kept my head down, not speaking or catching anyone's eye. Food was scarce and you had to be quick to get your share of the slops that were on offer, which meant I went hungry, and thirsty, because the water was yellow and smelled as if it had come from of a puddle in the stables at Bow.

---

[4] The smallest copper coin

On Sunday, I woke in the night, sweating and trembling from a nightmare. Bill, Nancy and Fagin, skins white and eyes popping from their sockets, were coming for me through a graveyard, while a bell tolled. A dreadful sound. The sound of death.

Then, I realised I was awake and the bell was real.

The cell was quieter than earlier, save for some of the more religious inmates muttering prayers and those who were awake shouting for them to shut their racket.

'St Sepulchre's!' I heard someone say, in a wavering voice, like Dickens' Ghost of Christmas Past. 'Hark, at the bell of St Sepulchre's!'

Newgate Prison is a short walk from the Old Bailey where Fagin was tried, and St Sepulchre's is a few yards from there. I knew it well, because what with all the lawyers and business gents rushing about, its narrow streets were good dodging territory and there were plenty of alleyways to make a quick getaway.

'What's St Sepulchre's?' whispered someone.

'When there's to be an execution,' droned the fellow, 'the sexton[5] comes to Newgate yard at midnight and rings a bell. A Jew is being executed in the morning.'

I never thought to ask for a name.

They called it the New Drop, for instead of standing the condemned person on a cart and

---

[5] Church caretaker

whipping-up the horses to leave him dangling in mid-air, he stood on a trapdoor, which the executioner opened by pulling a lever. All very modern, you'll agree.

Executions were carried out in public on Monday morning with men, women, and children going to the gallows for petty crimes as well as murder. I'd watched a few because they always drew a good crowd, especially for well-known villains, meaning there were rich pickings to be had from dipping pockets. I remember the last one I saw; a grey-haired man, quite grandfatherly, had been condemned for murder. He looked like a shopkeeper as he mounted the steps, hands tied behind him.

When asked if he had any last words, he stepped forward and said, 'I am as innocent as a new born babe!' Then he joined in with a vicar who was saying the Lord's Prayer. *Amen* was the signal, and no sooner had he uttered the word than the executioner yanked the lever and old chap disappeared through the floor, swinging like a pendulum in front of the crowd.

The drop always brought a cheer, but not that time. Silence swept over us and there weren't a dry eye in the crowd, with women weeping and men calling *shame!* An injustice had been done, and we knew it. I never went again, in spite of Fagin walloping me for missing the chance of making him richer. I made it up by strolling to Mayfair with Nancy and while she distracted a gent staggering out of Boodles Club, I relieved him of his purse, a gold watch and chain, and a blue silk kerchief with a coat of arms. He was a lord or some such important person, Fagin said. There were thirty guineas in that purse, which brought a smile to the old boy's evil face, but not before he'd slapped my head and threatened my life if he found out I'd kept anything back for myself.

Mr D doesn't describe Fagin's last moments, but the old villain must have heard the sexton's bell tolling for him, striking terror into his black heart. According to his version, which, I suppose, he got from the goalers, Mr Brownlow and Oliver were Fagin's last visitors, arriving a few hours before he was hanged, and wanting to know the whereabouts of certain papers a man called Monks had given him for safekeeping. Fagin had hidden them in the chimneybreast, and they proved that Oliver was due an inheritance of three thousand guineas, which Monks had been trying to diddle for himself. They might have been even richer if the old thief had let on where he kept his box of gold coins. I knew, and if I'd been free, I would have had it for myself.

Spending the weekend as a guest of Her Majesty in Newgate was how I came to see Fagin dangling there, and it fair upset me I can tell you. Even more than the grey-haired gent, and Fagin was no innocent.

Come Monday, with hardly any food or water in our bellies, four of us were chained together and marched away. As we came into the yard, I heard the trapdoor slam and the crowd cheer, never for a moment imagining that I was acquainted with the latest recipient of British justice.

Later, in Australia, I met a convict who'd seen it from start to finish. Fagin was well known, having done dirty business with every felon in the East End, the nobility and even royalty. When they brought him out, the yard was bursting with people, joking, quarrelling and pushing for a better view. They'd come to see him off in style. Not that he noticed for, so say, he was staring into space with a ridiculous smile on his face, like a man who didn't know what day it was. The lag said he'd gone mad. Well, who wouldn't, going to your grave with the crowd cheering like it was the Lord Mayor's Show? He didn't make a speech by all accounts, never protested his innocence, begged for mercy or, as some did, attack the executioner, William Calcraft, who had been a pie-seller at hangings until he got the job of executioner. Fagin knew him well and always bought a pie.

When the vicar asked him to join in the Lord's Prayer, he giggled hysterically and said he didn't know it. Well, he was Jewish, afterall.

Well, you could have knocked me down with a feather when I saw him swinging in the breeze not twenty paces from my face. I had no idea he'd even been arrested, let alone tried and sentenced. I half expected him to open his eyes, pull in his tongue and cuss at me for not working the crowd.

The Prince of Thieves, the King of Fences[6] was gone.

Fagin was dead.

I burst into tears.

You see, he was all I had.

---

[6] A fence receives and sells stolen goods

Chapter 3: The Deptford Hulks

It's a fair slog to Deptford in any weather. In the pouring rain with hands and feet shackled, and cold iron cutting your skin, it feels like eternity. The streets were swilling with mud mixed with slops from night-pots, and so-called honest folk, showing no sympathy, pelted us with rotting vegetables. We marched past the Mansion House where, no doubt, the Lord Mayor was drinking fine brandy with his hoity-toity banker chums, a fine bunch of thieves who made Fagin and Sikes look like angels, then south over Southwark Bridge and east along the Thames past the wharves where tall-masted ships were unloading cargoes from every corner of the world. North of the river, I felt at home. We seldom went south where it was dirt poor, and nothing but dockers and costermongers[7] with barely enough to feed their families, let alone have a few spare coppers for us thieves to pinch.

---

[7] A person who sells fruit and vegetables from a barrow

I felt the gaoler's truncheon twice, once on the head that left a lump the size of a goose egg after I stumbled and almost fell, the other a sharp jab in the ribs for asking where we were going.

'A lovely place,' he sneered, adding sadistically, 'a top-notch hotel called HMS Discovery.'

'You mean a ship,' I said. 'When does she sail?'

Anything, even the high seas, seemed better than the stinking ocean of mud that was South London.

'Sail? She don't sail nowhere,' he scoffed, as if talking to a gibbering idiot. 'Where have you been all your life? Ain't you heard of the *hulks*?'

I went cold at the very mention of the word.

The hulks were ancient warships no longer fit for battle or carrying cargo, stripped of their finery and turned into floating dungeons that lined the river from Greenwich down to Gravesend. Crime was rife in London in those days and there weren't enough prisons to lock up the guilty, until some bright cove in Parliament came up with idea of using old ships. I'd heard stories about what it meant to be sent to the hulks from a lag[8] who'd done seven years aboard a hellhole called the Justitia. He said that, by comparison, Newgate was soft and that he'd rather be topped than be sent back. Not that it stopped him burgling, and not a day went by when Fagin wasn't fencing[9] silverware for him.

---

[8] A convict or ex-convict
[9] Buying stolen property

In the pompous tones I'd used in court, I said, 'Forgive me, I do not understand, I am sentenced to transportation,' but I couldn't disguise the tremble in my voice. 'I am entitled to my rights!'

The gaoler was less than impressed. 'Don't you worry, my lucky lad,' he chortled, 'you'll be getting your rights soon enough in New South Wales, if you're not dead from typhus before you arrive!'

'New South Wales?' I said. One of Fagin's boys was from South Wales, Taffy we called him, and he'd walked all the way from Cardiff to London in bare feet. 'Surely, we are bound for Australia.'

'Botany Bay is where you're bound, in New South Wales, which is a part of Australia,' he said like a professor of geography. 'Never been myself, nor care to for that matter. There's nothing there 'cept convicts and sheep, and the seasons are upside down. Winter when it's summer and vice versa.'

Snow in August and sun in December were the last things on my mind, but I couldn't help wondering how it was possible.

We smelled the Hotel Discovery before we saw it. A stench worse than the foulest sewers that made us catch our breath. Bile rose in my throat and I thought I would vomit. When I caught sight of the ship through the fog and rain, fear gnawed at my guts like a pack of hungry rats. She was a ghost. Her rigging, or what was left of it, hung in shreds, and timbers that had gone unpainted for decades were crumbling from rot. Huts and tents had been built all over the decks, and filthy washing and the tattered bedding, hanging like battle-weary flags from ropes strung between them, reminded me of the slums around Fagin's den. Where great cannon had once roared through ports in her hull, smashing French and Spanish men-o'-war, now there were gaping holes closed by rusting prison bars. And coming from her, the dreadful nightmare sound of hundreds of clinking-clanking chains that made the rattling of our leg irons seem as sweet as tinkling birdsong.

Mr Dickens had some imagination when he wrote about the horrors visited upon the miser, Ebenezer Scrooge, in his book *A Christmas Carol*. It scared the britches off me the first time I read it, but even he couldn't have dreamed up the terrors that struck your heart at the first sight of the hulks.

'Home sweet home, my lucky lads,' the gaoler crowed, giving all four of us a stinging rap across the shins and pointing to the rowing boat beached on the black mud at the water's edge. 'Get a move on! I expect you'll be looking forward to a nice supper and a warm bed!'

It was too much to wish for. We squelched across up to our knees, leg irons tangling, causing each of us to take a header face first into the stinking mire. By the time we had clambered into the boat, without help from boatman, we were caked from head to foot and looking not unlike the black Dahomey[10] natives who were

---

[10] West African country now called Benin

fashionable as servants in posh houses in Mayfair and Belgravia.

Our goalers didn't follow, because there was no point. If anyone had tried to escape, all four of us would have gone to the bottom, saving the government a pile of money. Besides, it were no odds to them whether we lived or died.

No sooner had we reached Discovery's main deck by hauling ourselves up a rope net flung over the side, which is no easy task chained to three others, than a party of ill-uniformed gaolers pounced upon us, struck off our irons and ordered us to strip naked. Even in that freezing weather, there was no point objecting, for it would have brought fresh blows raining down on our heads or, as I later learned, finding yourself strapped to a frame and given a taste of the whip.

First, a demon barber sheared off our hair until our scalps were covered with stumpy ends and criss-crossed with bleeding cuts. Then they threw us into a huge wooden tub of icy water and forcibly scrubbed every inch of our bare skin with the coarse brooms used for cleaning the streets. Why they bothered, I'll never understand, only that it was one of the government's rules. The bath water was foul with greasy scum on top and what felt like thick slime beneath our feet. The brushes tore our skin, and by the time we were back on deck we were red raw and shivering with cold. We'd have come out cleaner if they'd thrown us into the Thames at Wapping, where nothing could live. Each of us was given a canvas jacket and trousers, soiled by the last wearers, mine five sizes too big, and ordered to sit on a bench where our ankles were shackled with ten pounds of iron hammered on without a care for breaking our bones. All ideas of escape were forgotten. Dive over the side and you were fish food.

When I complained that the gaoler searching our clothes had slit the lining of the pockets and discovered my silver sixpences they laughed, said it would cover my rent and, if I wanted to complain, I should put it in writing to Her Majesty, Queen Victoria, at whose pleasure I was now residing.

I'm not a big person and always wanted to be taller, but being short has advantages. Below decks there weren't enough room for a grown man to stand upright, and convicts learned to walk with a permanent stoop or brain themselves on the oak beams. Some, who had served five or more years, had bowed backs and never walked straight again. The beds were filthy, straw-filled mattresses side-by-side on the floor and not a blanket in sight. Years later, I learned that the government gave enough money for clothes, food and bedding, but the gaolers pocketed it, making themselves rich on the convicts' misery. There' are thieves wherever you look and, where there's a shilling to be made, finding an honest man is not easy.

We were fed that first night, but because we were the newest, we were last in a line that went right round the deck, which meant receiving the smallest portions. A one-eyed lag, who looked more like a murderer than a cook, and probably was, ladled ox-cheek soup from a saucepan into our bowls. It was stone cold by the time we got it, and so thin it looked like Thames water with greasy islands floating on the surface. A second cook dropped in a biscuit, green with mould and hard as brick. Since nothing had passed my lips for days, it tasted like manna from Heaven and I slurped it back like a famished wolf, licking my bowl until there was a danger of wearing away the metal. When there wasn't a trace left, I washed it down with a pint of beer. Four days a week we were given two pints each, which was a sight better than drinking river water filtered through dirty cloth. It's no wonder so many died.

As soon as I put my head on that mattress, I started to blub. I couldn't help it, lying there thinking about how I was going to spend the next seven years locked up in such conditions. The lag next to me put a stop to my noise by dealing me a backhander and warning that if I carried on I wouldn't live to see the morning.

'One more peep out of you and I'll wring your scrawny neck, understand?' he said, giving me another stinging slap that set my brain a–bonging like that bell at St Sepulchre's. I shut up quick. I knew those people, I'd lived amongst them, and understood what the devils were capable of.

One day passed much like another. We were woken by a bell, queued for a lump of bread and cup of water that served as breakfast, and then spent our time clanking around the deck or sitting on its damp boards waiting for the next meal, supper, twelve hungry hours away.

There was work ashore, but you had to have been locked up for years to get that privilege, and then share your wages with the goalers. Bribery was rife, and if you wanted your full quota of food and enough clothing to keep out the chill, you had to pay everyone from the captain down. Some cons received a few pennies and food from their families, which was far slimmer by the time they had all taken a slice. My money had gone, as had all my mates. There was always Oliver Twist, of course. Afterall, I did him a favour by introducing him to that respectable gentleman, Fagin, when he was starving and without a roof over his head. Not that I was expecting him to repay my kindness. So, I had nothing to buy extras. Inside a week, my ribs were showing and I looked like a starving street dog in Whitechapel.

A couple of times a week they took off the bodies of those who had died from disease or from despairing of ever being free. As I said, there are villains everywhere and even the dead made money for the goalers. Instead of being taken to the cemetery where criminals were buried, their corpses were sold to medical schools for dissection, while a coffin full of rocks was dropped into a pauper's grave. They were all in on it, the whole rotten lot, even the vicar.

Many times, I saw men punished. We were assembled on the deck to witness the wrongdoer given a taste of the cat, a whip with nine leather tails, each knotted at the end. Entertainment the guards called it, but we kept our eyes closed and tried not to listen to the screams. One offender, whose crime was a dirty leg iron, was sentenced to twenty lashes and passed out after eight, not that it stopped the bosun[11] from delivering the rest while his body hung limp and bleeding on the whipping frame. The other, who got double for talking back to an officer, screamed like the devil was after him, before going unconscious at seventeen. He wailed even louder when he was taken below and salt rubbed into the open wounds to keep them clean. He howled all night, though it didn't seem to keep many awake. They had seen and heard it too often, but it made me think twice about cheeking the goalers, I can tell you.

How many weeks we were locked-up on Discovery I can't say since the days came and went with nothing to break the boredom except for being forced to watch the bosun laying it on with a vengeance for serious crimes, like not wearing your cap straight, walking too quick or too slow, or looking a guard in the eye. We kept our heads down and tried to make ourselves invisible.

---

[11] Shortened form of boatswain, the officer responsible for a ship's equipment

Chapter 4: The Road to Portsmouth

After a while, time don't mean anything and I came to believe they had forgotten about us and transportation would never come. Then a rumour went around that special ships were being assembled in Portsmouth to carry us to Botany Bay. It turned out to be true, and the day came sooner than we thought. Before dawn had licked the sky downriver, the gaolers kicked us awake, told us to gather what few possessions we still had and, without food or drink, herded thirty of us into open carts and spiked our shackles to the floor.

We set off for Portsmouth, Pompey the old lags called it, in pouring rain and were to spend the next five days on wooden planks, bouncing on rutted roads, thin bodies bruising with every pothole. We slept on sodden grass, eating cold rations and never once washed or took off our wet clothes. Not that we had anything dry to put on.

Several times, coaches passed, with paying passengers wrapped in blankets inside, and convicts chained on top with the luggage.

'Travelling first class, them,' a guard laughed. 'Not that it'll get 'em to Australia any quicker.'

Whenever we passed through a village, people mocked us and threw rotten vegetables, which we plucked from the air and scoffed to stop the hunger pains. Mostly they made us sick adding to the misery inside the cart. One poor soul died on the third day but the gaolers didn't put his corpse off until the next, by which time it was giving off quite a stink.

Only once did anything happen to bring a smile to our faces, and that was when we stopped at an inn to change horses, and out came a gent in fine clothes who treated us to hot beef pie and a mug of ale. By his accent, he was Irish, a real Samaritan, like the chap in the Bible who helped a man set upon by thieves. I might be a thief, but I know my Bible because when Alfie Watchit taught me writing aboard the Lady Eugenia, it was all we had to read, though some of the pages were missing where cons had used them to roll baccy into smokes. There was sorrow in that man's eyes as he watched us wolfing the food and swilling real beer into our gullets. I don't know what he had to gain by it, but if I were ever to meet him again I'd tell him what his kindness did for us. Mind you, he had to bribe the guards a shilling each for the privilege of being allowed to help his fellow man.

'God bless you, M'lord!' cried a con, chin brown with gravy and a smile to light up London.

'I'm no lord,' said the gent, 'just a friend, and it is a small enough service I am able to do for you.'

'Your name, sir,' cried the chap, 'that I might remember your kindness when I am on the far side of the world.'

'Feargus O'Connor[12], Editor of the Northern Star, published in Leeds,' he says. 'And yours, sir?'

I'd never heard one of the upper classes address one of the lower, and a convicted criminal, as *sir*. It was a shock and clean took my mind off the food.

'John Colley, sir, of Harrow-on-the-Hill.' He stood and said proudly. 'I am sentenced to transportation for stealing a flask of laudanum to ease my wife's pain.'

'And what of your wife?'

'Dead, sir, of starvation, or so I heard while I was rotting in Deptford.'

O'Connor lowered his head as though he couldn't bear listening. When he looked up he doffed his hat and said, 'God bless you and keep you safe in that foreign land, and may you live the rest of your lives in peace.' There was a tear in his eye as he bowed and walked back to the inn.

For a while, we felt better with our stomachs full of hot food, until we set off and the heavens opened, drenching us all over again. It was as if

---

[12] Leader of the Chartist movement which worked ceaselessly for the rights and welfare of ordinary people

God had not heard a word that fine man had spoken.

Our first sight of the Portsmouth fleet was even more frightening than arriving at Deptford where, at least, you could see across the river. It was a busy port, and the main base of the Royal Navy.

To begin with there was a forest of tall-masted warships flying Her Majesty's colours then, further out, a line of hulks, filthy and grey like them on the Thames, and beyond another fleet with furled sails, tight rigging and no shanties, washing lines or prison bars. These were ocean-going vessels, ready for the six months or more it would take to reach Australia. I couldn't imagine how far that was.

I turned to the geezer next to me. 'Will they bring us back when we've done our time?'

'Most stay there, so I've been told,' he said. 'Me, I'm a lifer, leaving behind a missus and six young 'uns, so it don't make no difference to me. But who'll take care of 'em? Tell me that, who'll take care of them now?' With that, he broke down in tears and I couldn't help but wonder if his little children would find themselves in the grip of a villain like Fagin, learning bad ways and being forced to steal for their supper. Then he started beating himself with his chains and bawling, 'I took that piglet only because my babies were starving. What's a pig to a rich man? I'm a mason, I could've worked off the debt, however long it took. Who'll take care of 'em now?'

'Shut your mouth!' bawled a guard. 'You ought to have thought of that before you took up thieving.'

I ain't the sentimental sort, as you'll have gathered, but I couldn't hold back a tear and went as far as putting my arm round that man's heaving shoulders while he sobbed into my jacket. For a minute, I couldn't help thinking that my own father, of whom I have no recollection good or bad, might have found himself in the same desperate state of affairs and delivered me to Fagin's doorstep.

Since being sentenced, I'd heard a lot of people talking about justice, mostly well-fed types wearing fine togs and riding about in carriages. But where was the justice in packing that man off to Australia? Didn't it make matters worse, sending him to the other side of the world, leaving a family who'd probably have to turn to crime to survive? To my mind, it was making seven criminals out of one. I've no education, but it's common sense that if you let a man earn a crust he'll be too busy working to go thieving, and wouldn't need to anyway.

I won't bore you with all the details of boarding the hulk where we were held for the next week, because it was much the same as Deptford except that the gaolers were supervised by red-jacketed marines with rifles. We were rowed out from a pier thronging with men, women and children come to say farewell to fathers and sons, many with small sacks and bundles containing food, money, clothing and tobacco. A few convicts, like the carpenter who'd spoken to Mr Feargus O'Connor, were craftsmen and their wives had brought the tools of their trade, which they were allowed to take with them. I haven't mentioned women convicts, but there were some and even husbands and wives doing time together. They boarded from another pier. I didn't see it myself but some lags swore they'd seen children, real little 'uns, seven or eight years old though, as far as I could see, I was the youngest by years. And whose fault was that, save my own stupid self?

As we were pressed into longboats, the wailing became louder as wives and children clung to husbands and fathers and had to be torn away by the goalers who left the poor devils sobbing on the planks. It was enough to break the hardest heart and, at that moment, I was happy not to have a mother seeing me off to who knew where.

Then it was the same as before, unshackling, bathing, scrubbing, barbering, re-shackling and being led below decks to where we were to sleep. It was no picnic, but after the journey from London it was like lodging in one of those posh gentlemen's clubs in Pall Mall, except that their members don't wear leg irons. It was warmer, there was food, clean water and our belongings weren't being stolen. Not that I had any.

It was a Sunday when we were moved from the hulk to our transport. I know because the sun was shining and the church bells were ringing. If it had been London, crowds would have been out in the parks and the pickings would have brought a smile to Fagin's horrible face.

We boarded from the ocean side and as we passed beneath the great bowsprit I looked up at the ship's name in freshly painted white letters.

'Lady Eugenia,' read an educated lag they called Professor Tom. 'Sounds nice, don't it? More like someone's sister than a prison.'

She wasn't a man-o-war, but a converted merchantman fitted out with berths, two-high, set in rows against the hull with an aisle down the middle. The only ventilation was from hatches in the deck covered by thick iron grilles. The stairway through which we emerged on to the deck had a cage built over it, with a gate big enough for only one person to squeeze through at a time, and all the while we were on deck the ship's gunners trained cannon on us. All thoughts of mutiny or escape were hopeless and anyone trying it would surely be blown to pieces.

Chapter 5: The Atlantic Ocean

We sailed the following morning with several hundred of us locked below decks. It was dark and it was the cries of sailors clambering into the rigging, and the crack of billowing sails that alerted us to the fact that we were moving. We saw nothing of our departure and no sooner were we out of port and into the Channel, than the whole lot of us were vomiting what little food we had in our stomachs and rolling around like we were at death's door.

The next day, with land out of sight, our chains were struck off and after cleaning up the vile mess swilling about on the floors, we were allowed on deck for exercise and fresh air.

At noon the marines, a tough looking bunch, assembled us on the main deck to be addressed by Captain Grant, a grey-haired man in his fifties, attired in navy blue with plenty of gold, whose weather-beaten face showed he was a man who had lived his life at sea.

A deep hush fell as he stepped to the rail.

'You are prisoners at the pleasure of Her Majesty, Queen Victoria, sentenced to transportation to Australia. As captain of the Lady Eugenia, I am Her Majesty's representative and all-powerful in matters of the law, discipline and punishment of wrongdoers. The voyage will be long and hard, but I am a fair man. You will not be shackled without good reason and will be allowed such freedom as the limited space permits. You will be free to walk the main deck under the scrutiny of the marines by day, and at night you will be locked below. You will receive a proper share of rations and be permitted to fish. But, I warn you, do not transgress. Do not steal, fight or attempt escape or mutiny. All offences will be harshly punished.'

I didn't know what to make of it. Some of the lags talked to the crew who said that Captain Grant had a reputation as a fair man and, unlike others, never dished out punishment without good reason. In any case, the best advice was always to keep your nose clean and steer clear of trouble.

And so we settled down to the next chapter in our lives, which, after what we'd been through, didn't seem too bad. Easier than on the hulks anyway. The weather was chilly, but the sun was shining and we quickly found our sea legs. We washed and scrubbed the decks, sewed sails and were taught how to splice rope. No one bothered if we chattered, sung, danced or laughed as we went about our business. There was plenty of grub, not the finest and mainly brine beef, commonly known as salt horse. If the butchers in Portsmouth were as crooked as those in Deptford, much of it probably was horse. We ate it with rice or peas and, sometimes, there was even a bit of plum pudding as a treat. The truth is, I'd never had so much food in my life, and half a pint of port wine each night to wash it down. Three times a week we had to drink a horrible mixture of lime juice, sugar and vinegar which, the ship's surgeon said, would stop us getting scurvy and keep us healthy. Several on board were skilled fishermen and, with lines made by picking canvas apart, and hooks carved from bones and baited with leftover salt horse, they pulled out some fair sized beasts. I'd never tasted fish until I traded my nightly ration of port for a juicy piece as long and as thick as my finger, roasted over a brazier on the deck. At first, I wasn't keen on the smell, but once I'd popped it in my mouth and it had melted away like butter I couldn't get enough.

We weren't quite so keen on eating when we sailed into the Bay of Biscay, where the waves were bigger than St Paul's Cathedral and crashed over the Lady Eugenia, making us howl with terror. We were locked below, clinging to our bunks for dear life as water rushed in through the hatches, down the staircases and flowing across the floor like a river as the ship was tossed about like a toy boat on the Serpentine. I don't pray, but for the three days we were in that unholy place, when there was no difference between day and night, I never stopped. Nor did those around me.

We weren't allowed knives except for those issued with our food and then collected afterwards, but it didn't stop the lags making all manner of ornaments and useful things from scraps of bone and pieces of wood. Fish were more plentiful in the warmer water and, soon, there was an abundance of fat, silvery Bonitos that seemed to want to jump on to our hooks. We even ate shark meat, which judging by the rows of teeth in the mouths of those monsters was better than them eating you.

Some of the men formed themselves into choirs and sang as if they hadn't a care in the world. Perhaps they hadn't. We were unsure what the future held, but we were alive, fattening up, with nothing to worry us. Some of the older men, who'd left families behind, were morose until they realised there was nothing they could do about their plight and settled down. There were a few who didn't, who went to the rail and stared at the horizon all day talking mumbo jumbo to themselves. At night, they lay in their bunks staring at the ceiling. I think not knowing what was happening to their families drove them mad. When a con tried to end it all by jumping into the sea, there was no attempt to save him and we had to watch his bobbing head disappearing in our wake.

There were plenty of Bibles on board, donated by good Christian folk to help us through the journey. And help they did. I learned to read, but they had plenty of other uses, which distressed the missionaries who accompanied us when the lags took them apart and turned them into cards for gambling.

There was less trouble than on the hulks and the cat o' nine tails was seldom used though, from time to time, the bosun carried it on his rounds, snapping her tails in the air as a warning of what we would receive if we dared step out of line.

The Lady Eugenia, bound for Botany Bay, would cross the Atlantic Ocean, putting in at the Canary Islands and Cape Verde Islands to take on fresh water and supplies, before sailing to Rio de Janeiro in South America. From there we were to cross the Atlantic in the opposite direction to Cape Town on the southernmost tip of Africa. I could not imagine the distance we were to travel. Sixteen thousand miles the crew said. *Sixteen thousand!* I'd walked from Watford to Whitechapel, which weren't thirty, and that was enough for me. I could not grasp the number. Was it as far as the moon? Or further? I could see the moon, but I couldn't see Australia.

'Why do we not go there directly,' I asked a junior officer, who was an affable sort of chap.

'We are a sailing ship,' says he, as if speaking to the village idiot, 'and must go where the winds blow best and the currents are most favourable. Sometimes that means sailing in the opposite direction.'

The truth was I had no idea about winds and currents or where any of the places were. Even when he drew me a map, I was none the wiser. You don't learn much about the world picking pockets in London.

'And supposing the winds and currents carry us as quick as they might, how long will the journey take?' I asked.

Well, you could have knocked me down with a feather when he says the voyage could be up to two hundred days. Perhaps Australia was further than the moon.

From Cape Town we were to sail for Botany Bay, putting in only once at Hobart in Van Diemen's Land[13], which I didn't like the sound of one little bit.

After the Bay of Biscay, the weather had gradually become calmer and warmer because Africa, which I *had* heard of, was off to our left hand side, or port as seafarers call it. It was where black chaps came from. One of Fagin's boys was from Africa but couldn't remember anything of it except that it was warm and green, not like London.

---

[13] Tasmania, the big island off the south coast of Australia

In the Canary Islands, we anchored outside a harbour called Santa Cruz, and how I wished we could have gone ashore to that sunny, green place with a cone shaped mountain rising into the clouds at its centre. It looked nothing short of paradise and I envied the crew as they set off for visits ashore.

Small boats came out with the supplies, the seamen brown as berries from the sun and chattering in a language I'd never heard, though a few in the crew could speak it.

Some of the more trusted convicts were allowed to help with the loading until one, John Carpenter, smuggled himself onto a supply boat and escaped to the islands. We cheered when we heard, but soon changed our tune when they locked everyone below until we left port, after which his name was mud. A search party caught him after two days and he was brought back in shackles with great lumps on his face where he'd been beaten. As soon as we were at sea, they gave him one hundred lashes from the cat o' nine tails in front of the whole crew. When they cut him down, his back was as raw as a side of beef on Smithfield Market.

Because of howling gales we didn't stop at Cape Verde, and never caught so much as a glimpse of the place through the driving rain.

One day, standing at the rail, it occurred to me that just like rich folk from the West End we were on a world tour. The only difference was we never saw anything save the sea.

Two days past Cape Verde the weather became hotter and more humid and we spent our days and nights bathed in sweat. Worse, the population of the Lady Eugenia grew as rats, cockroaches and fleas bred in huge numbers until every corner of the ship was infested. The crew tried burning them out with gunpowder and we dosed everything with tar oil, but to no avail. To cap it all, the bilges[14], which were filled with seawater, urine, dead rats and every other kind of filth, began stinking to high heaven so that we were left gasping and vomiting with almost every breath.

It didn't stop there.

When we reached that piece of ocean called the Doldrums there was not a breath of wind for a week and we lay becalmed on an ocean as flat as glass. Our lives were made worse when the Captain rationed food and water. Four men died that week and were buried at sea.

Eventually, the wind got up, lifting our spirits, and we were under way for Rio.

Having had no schooling, except at Fagin's academy for young villains, the names of countries meant nothing, nor did the Equator, which we were due to cross with great ceremony. Everyone, crew, convicts and paying passengers, believe it or not there were paying passengers with servants on board, were excited by the prospect. By then, I was mates with Alfie Watchit who bunked on the floor near me and was a celebrity amongst the

---

[14] The lowest part of ship where dirty water collects

felons because his case, in which he had forged thousands of pounds worth of government bonds, had been the talk of England. There were even etching of him in the newspapers.

So, I said, 'What's this Equator, Alfie? It sounds important.'

'It's a line round the middle of the earth,' he says, swirling a finger in the air. 'Halfway between the North Pole and the South Pole. When we cross it there will be a fine celebration.'

'I shall look forward to that,' I said, wondering what a line in the middle of the sea might actually look like. '*Exactly* what is it? Is it a thin piece of land going all the way round, or what?'

Alfie laughed fit to burst. 'It is imaginary,' he replied. 'You cannot see it.'

It wasn't the answer I was expecting, because how could it be there, if it wasn't?

'Well, if it can't be seen, how does the Captain know it's there and how will he know we've crossed it?'

'The Captain knows all right. You've seen him up there,' he nodded towards the quarterdeck, 'looking through that brass instrument at midday when the sun is overhead. It's called a sextant and it allows him to calculate the exact position of the ship on the ocean. How else would he be able to find Australia instead of going round in circles?'

Funny, living in London makes you think you know everything, but in the few months since being nicked I'd learned that there was more in the world than I could ever have imagined and most of it wasn't in that damp, dirty, smoky city.

Alfie said. 'Do you know your letters?'

As a matter of fact, I did know a few. 'I can recognise 'em from picking initials out of handkerchiefs with a needle,' I told him.

'Such a skill,' he remarked. 'Can you write your name?'

'I make a cross. Don't everyone?'

'Many people can write their name.'

'The rich, who've had schooling,' I said, 'but what use is it to a convicted criminal like me?'

'You can find everything in books,' he said. 'I never went to school, but I was apprenticed to a silversmith who taught me. I could teach you.'

With a swagger, I said, 'And what good's reading and writing when it comes to putting food on the table. I've got other talents.' With that, I slipped my fingers into his pocket and dodged the purse he kept there. He never felt a thing.

'It's them talents what got you here,' he said, coming over all concerned and fatherly.

'And got me this!' I opened my fist and showed him his purse.

'Why you young devil!' With that he walloped my head so hard I was seeing stars for a full minute. 'Best you don't go trying that here. You've no need for it and there's hard men would see you take your last breath for less.' He snatched away the purse and tucked it inside his shirt. He'd learned a lesson, too.

That was how I came to know my letters. Alfie was a good teacher and I surprised him and myself by being a willing pupil and taking to it like a duck to water. There were no books except the Bible, which had some big words that even Alfie couldn't say. Not that it stopped me understanding the stories. Some were real interesting, like that Noah chap who got flooded with his animals when water covered the world. I had no problem believing it since we'd been at sea for weeks and never caught sight of land. Then there was Jonah who was swallowed by a whale. I would never have believed it possible until we saw those great beasts, some as big as our ship, blowing out fountains of water.

One day, there was quite a hubbub after the Captain and his officers had gathered to observe the noon sun through their sextants and pronounced that at four o'clock that very day we would cross the Equator.

You would have thought that Queen Victoria in person was joining us for supper the way the crew began scampering about like children.

The regular sailors dressed up as mermaids, with long blonde hair made from the hemp used to make the ship's timbers watertight. The newer ones, who hadn't crossed the equator before, were lined up with knees knocking to receive what was coming their way.

At four o'clock the ship's bell rang and Neptune, King of the Deep, climbed over the rail on to the deck. He was quite a sight, covered from head to toe in a suit of fish-scales embroidered with seaweed, shells and starfish, and a beard that reached the ground. As far as I could see, old Neptune bore a striking resemblance to the bosun. Upon his command, the mermaids fell upon the new boys, held them down and scoured them with soapy brushes. They squealed like piglets as their hair was shaved off before they were dunked in a tub of sea water filled with the eight-legged monsters they called squids, that squirmed all over their bodies. It reminded me of boarding the hulks at Dartford, and we laughed at their plight until our sides ached fit to bust. Then rum was issued and they danced through the night to music from banjo, drum and squeezebox.

Personally, I couldn't understand what the fuss was about. Crossing a line no one could see didn't make sense. The world gets stranger, the more you see of it.

Strange to say, but although I was a convict and life was hard, I was happy because I knew where I stood. There was no running from the law or getting backhanded by Fagin and Sikes for not stealing enough. My stomach was full, the air was fresh and, if you used your common sense and kept out of trouble, it weren't half bad.

But, as I've learned to my cost, there's always someone who'll come along and spoil it.

Chapter 6: Mutiny

Most of the lags were prepared to make the best of the voyage and take what was coming to them in Australia, but there were a few real bad 'uns who wanted nothing other than to cause trouble. Not that they had anything to gain by it, they just didn't know any better and to them life was meaningless without thieving, fighting or murdering.

After we'd been locked down on the night of crossing the line, and the mermaids were still singing and dancing drunkenly on the deck above our heads, a group of lags gathered in a corner by the light of a flickering candle to mutter about the injustice of their situation. Alfie used to say that the devil makes work for idle hands, and there was always talk of stealing extra rations or selling tobacco and rum. But never before had I heard talk of mutiny, taking over the ship, a crime so serious they'd carry you back to London in chains and top you at Newgate as an example to them who'd go against Her Majesty's Royal Navy. That night, there was anger in their voices because one, by the name of Hobbs, had been backhanded by a guard for insolence. Huddled in a grim-faced circle, hatred was burning fierce, and they were serious about revenge.

Mutiny.

At the mention of it, those with any sense crept off to their bunks, turned their backs and closed their ears, wanting no part of what was being planned, or to be seen in the company of the plotters. Alfie was nervous and told me to get to my bunk. I, being what I am, couldn't hold back from sneaking into the shadows close by and bending an ear to what they were saying. Curiosity killed the cat, goes the old saying. Well, as you'll learn, it very nearly killed me.

'We can do it!' Hobbs whispered, his coarse voice rasping through the darkness. 'We can take this ship and sail her anywhere in the world. We'll disappear never to be found. We shall be free to do as we please for the rest of our days. I heard tell of a ship called the *Bounty* where those who did the same sailed off to paradise in what they call the South Seas. They were never found.'

'And who shall be the Lady Eugenia's master,' snorted one of his mates. 'Can you sail her, Hobbs? Do you have an understanding of ropes and sails and navigating by the sun and stars? Not to mention storms or putting in at places for food and water.'

Hobbs ignored him. 'We shall set the marines and officers adrift in a longboat and force the Captain to obey our commands on peril of death. The crew will do as we say.'

'The marines will blast us to pieces.'

'Not if we do it at night when there are only two on patrol,' said Hobbs.

'And all while we are locked below,' piped up one called No Nose Jack, on account of it having been sliced off in a tavern fight leaving two gaping holes in the front of his face. 'A fine trick if you can pull it off.'

'We'll get the keys to the armoury,' says Hobbs. 'The marines will not be expecting anything and will probably be dozing. Every man who's with us shall have a musket and cutlass.'

'And just how, may I be so bold as to ask, are we to come by the keys?' says a lag resembling a weasel. 'It's an impossible plan, Hobbs. They'd be missed as soon as it came to lock up.'

That foxed Hobbs and he had no answer until a voice said, 'If you can lay hands on the keys I can make copies.' It was a chap called Springer, who usually kept himself to himself and didn't seem the sort to be involved with the harder criminals.

'And what do you know of such matters?' says Hobbs in a mocking tone.

'I was sentenced for cracking the safe of a well-known West End solicitor, and would have got away with it had I not been shopped to the law by the city rogue who employed me in the first place,' he said. 'I am a locksmith, the best, and the keys that open the doors on this vessel are child's play compared with that safe. It can be done.'

The group murmured approval.

'Where are the keys kept?' asked Hobbs, excited that his plan for freedom seemed a pace nearer.

'The guard has 'em on a ring with others, which he keeps in his coat pocket when on deck.'

'How long will you need it, Springer?'

'If I am well prepared, five minutes and no longer.'

'Then, it's obvious! What we need is a dip, someone with velvet fingers who can pick a pocket.'

I had been listening intently up until that point when it suddenly dawned on me that I was more than qualified for the job in hand, and should have taken Alfie's advice and gone to my bed, before they realised I was listening. I shrunk deeper into the shadows wishing I could sneak off without being spotted.

'That's it!' said No Nose. 'A guard won't miss 'em for the few minutes it takes Springer to work his magic.'

'And who will do the job?' says Hobbs. 'From what I see, there's none amongst us with the skill.'

Out of the darkness came a throaty chuckle. It frightened me, for somehow I knew what was coming next.

'What about 'im, hiding like a rat in the corner?'

The man hadn't spoken before, and I had the feeling I knew him, yet couldn't put my finger on it. Now, with candlelight flickering on his face, I realised that without the beard I would have recognised him straight off.

'You mean young Dodger?' said Hobbs, glowering at me. 'He's a cheeky one I'll grant you, but he don't do nothing 'cept talk to old Alfie and read the Bible.'

'Take it from me, the boy's a dip,' he said to the group. 'And a good 'un if memory serves me right. It's how he came by the name Artful Dodger.'

I remembered his name, Willis, a burglar and an accomplice of Sikes. I'd seen him at Fagin's place when he'd come to sell the night's plunder.

'I've seen him operate,' went on Willis as every eye turned to me. 'Fingers as nimble as a Bond Street seamstress. Come here, you.'

I looked wide-eyed and innocent. 'Me?' I asked as if butter wouldn't melt in my mouth.

Willis was having none of it. 'Stop your tom-foolery and get over here afore I take my fist to you.'

Reluctantly, I made my way to the corner where No Nose grabbed my wrist and dragged me down. They crowded around like a pack of hungry dogs.

'Are you a dip? Speak, afore I give you a walloping.'

Believe me, I wanted no part of their plan. Dipping in Mayfair is one thing, picking a pocket under the noses of marines with guns is a different altogether, though I wasn't in a position to say so.

'He was one of Fagin's lads,' said Willis to mutterings of approval since Fagin was one of London's most famous criminals and well thought of for the fine apprenticeship he gave his boys.

'That's a good reference, no messing,' said Springer. 'You overheard. Can you do it? Can you get the keys?'

'I'm out of form,' I said off-handedly. 'I ain't done dipping for ages. Besides, I was never very good. I got nicked and ended up here, didn't I? There's many that's better, and I wouldn't want to ruin your plans.'

Not best pleased with me for making him look a fool, Willis, took me by the shirt and pulled me towards him. He was strong and it hurt.

'Take care, Dodger,' he hissed through ugly brown teeth, his stinking breath hot on my face. 'I know your work and if'n you want to keep that pretty face of your'n, you'll do as you're told, get me?' He ran a finger across his throat to remind me of my fate if I played them false.

These were real villains, who wouldn't think twice about carrying out their threats.

'You'll do it and do it proper,' says Hobbs. 'I'll tell you when. Until then, not a word, understand?'

Alfie caught me the next day and pushed me into a corner where we couldn't be heard. There was no denying he was angry.

'I heard everything,' he hissed. 'Did I not warn you? I know what those madmen are planning and if you're with them you will surely meet a bad end.'

'Nothing I can't handle,' I said, acting brave as a bull, but knowing he was right.

'Then tell them *no*! Say you will not do it.'

'If I do, they will kill me for sure.'

'Go to the Captain. Tell him what you know. They'll be clapped in irons and he'll protect you.'

'Shop 'em,' I said, not believing my ears. 'You mean peach? Peach on 'em? What do you think I am?'

Fagin had drummed it into us that peaching was the ultimate sin for which you could never be forgiven. If we were caught, we were never to peach, even if it meant being publicly topped at Newgate.

'You have to,' says Alfie.

'Not me,' says I. 'I'm no nark! I never peached at my trial and I'll not do it now. I'd rather die than be known for that.'

'So you will if you go along with them,' he says. He had become like a father to me and there was a tear in his eye.

'I shall do what they want,' I said. 'I shall dip the key but I won't go with them.'

'If they take the ship we shall all be with them whether we like it or not. We shall all be caught and hanged. The innocent and the guilty. I beg you, Jack, reconsider before it is too late,' he implored.

I could face him no longer, and ran upstairs to the deck. Hobbs's gang were gathered at the rail and spotted me as I came out of the cage. Hobbs broke away and strolled in my direction.

'Be ready, Dodger,' he hissed from the corner of his mouth as he passed by. 'Be ready, and try no tricks or it'll be the worse for you.'

After that, I could have sworn that every marine had his eye on me, just as if they knew what was going on. Even if had I wanted to take Alfie's advice and approach one of the officers, it would have been impossible, for that bunch of desperados never let me out of their sight for a second.

We were a week from Rio. Days had drifted by and lifting the keys had not been mentioned. They were cutting it fine and I almost came to believe they had given up on the idea, until Hobbs took my elbow and marched me to the rail. My stomach turned over worse than a bout of seasickness.

'In a few minutes, No Nose and Willis will come out of the cage and speak to the guard. They will be noisy and ask him to settle an argument. The key ring is in his left pocket. While he is distracted, you will take it. As I pass by, you will drop it into my pocket. When I go below, follow at a respectable distance so that the guards suspect nothing. Now get yourself into position.' He squeezed my arm so that I winced with pain. 'And I warn you, Artful Dodger, try nothing that will cause our plan to fail.' With that, he gave me a hard shove towards the cage.

I lurked near the bars trying to look as if nothing was afoot until No Nose and Willis came on deck arguing about how many days we'd been at sea and how many more it was to Botany Bay.

My old street instincts took over and it felt as if I was back in the West End dodging rich gents for their wallets. I have to admit it was quite a thrill. The guard's pocket was large and baggy, easy pickings for a chap of my talent. As I watched them get the guard's attention, my fingers itched, eager to do the deed. I spotted Hobbs and nodded that I was ready. In three quick paces I was behind the guard with my back to his, slipping my hand into his pocket. It was like taking sweetmeats from a baby. Hobbs's timing was perfect and as he passed, I slipped him the key and strolled off as if it was Hyde Park on a Sunday morning.

A minute later I found Hobbs and Springer in a corner below deck kneeling over a cloth upon which were laid two boxes filled with what looked and smelled like soap. It was good stuff, too, and probably nicked off a passenger by a servant, who had sold it to a sailor, who had sold it on to the gang. As I said, there's money to be made everywhere, even on a prison ship in the middle of the Atlantic Ocean.

There were four keys on the ring. Springer knew which was which and chose the largest, wiping it clean and pressing it firmly into the soap.

He removed it carefully, turned it over and pressed the opposite face before removing any traces of soap. He did the same with a smaller key, which I suspected, fitted the lock to the armoury.

He handed me the ring.

'Tip the wink to Hobbs and No Nose and they'll distract the guard while you put 'em back.'

I slipped the keys into my trouser pocket. The ring was large and it was a tight fit. By then, I'd gone off the whole idea and couldn't wait for it to be over.

I went up the ladder like a squirrel after nuts and emerged from the cage. Hobbs and No Nose were standing near the mast. Upon seeing me they headed for the guard and starting pestering him all over again. As soon as they had his attention I moved in, hand in pocket.

The keys snagged on the ragged cloth.

I yanked hard and they came free. I lost my grip and they clattered to the wooden deck.

The guard whirled and I saw the backs of Hobbs and Springer disappearing before the guard laid me out good and proper with his truncheon.

And that was me, banged to rights for a second time.

How long I was out, I haven't a clue. When I came round, I was on the boards of a cell, hands and feet in irons, head aching as if a galloping coach and four had run me down. I didn't need anyone to tell me that I was in a bad fix.

How I wished I'd listened to Alfie when he had warned me to go to bed but, as you'll have gathered, that was my character, cleverer than all the rest put together. A know-all you might say, no one to blame for my plight but myself.

What little light was filtering through a porthole had gone by the time two marines came to get me. Each took an arm and without as much as a *good evening, Mr Dawkins* dragged me out, and up a flight of steps to the deck. The moon was out and the convicts had been locked below. They hauled me to a pair of doors with frosted glass panes a-glow with light from a lamp within. Two more marines stood sentry. At our arrival, one rapped the door.

'Enter!'

The Captain, an officer on either side, sat at his table, the guard I'd dipped standing to attention at one end.

'The convict, Dawkins, sir!' shouted a marine like the Captain was deaf and I was Napoleon or some such dangerous person.

The Captain didn't stand on ceremony.

'You are accused of theft. How do you plead?'

When I said nothing, a marine elbowed me hard and said, 'Answer the Captain, you thieving scum.'

'Guilty or not guilty?' asked the Captain.

'Not guilty,' I piped, not confident that they were going to take my word for it. One of the officers wrote it in a journal.

The Captain sighed. 'This guard accuses you of attempting to steal his keys. For what reason?'

'I never was,' I said, wide-eyed and innocent. 'I was coming from below and the first I knew, those keys was rattling about on the deck. He must have dropped 'em. Then he walloped me on the nut and I was a-goner. I know nothing else.'

'The convicts Hobbs, Willis and Springer are they known to you?'

'They bunk nearby,' I said. 'As for knowing 'em, well, they ain't exactly good mates of mine.'

'I suggest that you were stealing the keys as part of an attempt at mutiny,' says the Captain who, I could see, was getting angry with me. 'Fortunately the plot has been thwarted. But you could not have been the mastermind, so I ask again, were Hobbs, Willis and Springer your co-conspirators?'

They had me in chains, and perhaps the others were also locked up, but they hadn't realised that I was putting the keys back, because I was being accused of attempting to steal them, which meant they didn't know they had been copied.

'I repeat,' barked the Captain. 'Were those men, or others you might name, your co-conspirators?'

Never peach, mates or not. That was Fagin's law and I couldn't get it out of my mind.

'I am being made a scapegoat,' I said. 'Them keys fell out of his pocket. That's all I know and you cannot blame me for another man's carelessness.' Brass-faced but with twitching bowels, I went on, 'You've got the wrong man, sir. I am innocent.' With that, I threw out my chest, raised my chin and tried to look the British hero.

The Captain seemed disappointed.

'You are young and I believe the victim of these men,' he said, his tone softer, 'but if you will not admit your crime I cannot protect you and the law must take its course.' He sat back for a moment waiting for me to change my mind. When I said nothing, he said. 'Very well, you leave me no option. I find you guilty of the offence with which you have been charged and you are hereby sentenced to forty lashes to be delivered on the morrow afternoon before the crew and convicts. I am a fair man and will give you until that time to reconsider. Name the others involved in this plot and the number of lashes you receive will be halved. Take him away.'

I was still bawling that they had the wrong man when they tossed me into the cell where I was to stay without food or water.

I never slept a wink that night. I ask you, who would with that hanging over them? Even if I turned nark and peached, I was still going to get twenty strokes. Judging by what I'd witnessed at Deptford and the lashing of John Carpenter, I would be unconscious by the time I taken half a dozen, so what odds did it make how many I took. If I didn't turn that vile gang in, at least I'd be able to hold my head up in front of the lags I was going to spend the next seven years with.

I don't know what time it was when a mid-shipman, who couldn't have been much older than me, entered the cell.

'Captain Grant requests your answer,' says he, like he was master and commander of the vessel. 'Will you name those who put you up to this?' Despite his age, he had the plummy voice of those posh gents you see swanning about in Belgravia. Good breeding they call it, but I ain't so certain.

I was tempted, that was for sure, and it was on the tip of my tongue to blurt out the names and be fingered for a scab. But when I looked at that young chap, all pink skinned with blonde hair and looking the double of Oliver Twist, I wasn't about to give him the satisfaction of seeing me turn coward.

'Tell your Captain he is mistaken,' I said. 'Them keys fell on the deck without my aid. He is punishing an innocent man.'

He said nothing and, hands clasped behind his back like a real officer, strode from the cell, a marine slamming the door behind him.

I started to cry.

First a blub, then tears streaming down my face, shoulders heaving with every sob.

It wasn't long before a drumbeat started on the deck and the mid-shipman returned with two marines. This time he didn't speak, just motioned the marines to take me.

I pulled myself together and stopped crying though my legs were wobbling like a tub of jellied eels. I couldn't stand alone, so they dragged me across the deck to the main mast where the crew were gathered to one side of a square, the convicts on the other three, marines with cocked muskets facing them.

In the front line stood Hobbs, No Nose, Springer and Willis, with faces of stone, fearful that at any minute I would blurt out their names and they would find themselves in my place. Strangely, the sight of those rotten men stiffened my spine and I was not about to let them see that I could not take the medicine.

Shrugging the marines off, I placed my feet apart and stood square on the deck without their aid, facing the bosun who stood before an upright grille, a sack in his left hand. I knew what it contained. The cat o' nine tails was waiting for me.

I caught sight of Alfie who had tears in his eyes, before they triced me to the grille, spreading me out across its bars like a kipper ready for smoking. I never made a sound as the first officer read out the charges and the punishment.

'Forty lashes!' he pronounced.

The bosun stepped forward, grasped my collar and tore my shirt straight down the back. I never saw him slip the cat out of the bag nor run it through a wet rag to make it supple.

'Lay on with a will, bosun,' cried the first officer.

I braced myself, and before I knew it, those tails were whistling through the air, biting into my ribs.

I felt no pain. At first, that is.

I suppose it was the shock.

Then a thousand knives wielded by a thousand devils were plunged through my skin at once.

'One!' cries the bosun.

I screamed so loud that they must have heard me in Portsmouth.

Before I knew it, he had delivered another.

'Two!' I heard.

'Three!' he shouted.

'Four!'

How many I took before I was mercifully overcome by unconsciousness I cannot say, but it weren't too many more.

They were sloshing me down with buckets of seawater when I came round to see my own blood swilling over my feet. The marines were at my shoulders, unstrapping my hands and Alfie was whispering in my ear.

'I shall look after you, Jack, don't worry. Close your eyes. Close your eyes and let yourself go.'

That's all I remember of that terrible affair until I woke face down on my bunk, back burning like Lucifer had lit a fire on it. Alfie was kneeling beside me, stroking my brow and telling me to be brave while he treated my wounds to prevent infection. I don't know which was worse, the cat or the treatment.

Two cons grabbed my wrists and two more my ankles, stretching me out to keep me flat. The pain cannot be described.

'Do not let him loose,' Alfie told them. 'I'm sorry, Jack, but this is necessary and it will be painful.'

With that, he shoved a roll of leather into my mouth to stop me biting off my tongue. Then his hands were rubbing salt into the wounds. He was right. It hurt. I screamed some more, then there was blackness.

Later, Alfie told me that I had raved for days, crying out for Fagin and Nancy, cursing the day I found Oliver and had taken him back, though I have no knowledge of it. When I finally came to, I was still face down and he was waiting with a bowl of gruel and a wooden spoon to feed me.

'The Captain gave me permission to stay with you day and night,' he said. 'You will be in pain for some time but your wounds are not infected. You will heal. Be sure of it.'

I often think about what might have happened if our positions had been reversed and Alfie had been the one with a back like a piece of raw beef. I would have been all high and mighty, telling him what a fool he'd been and asking why he hadn't listened to me. But he didn't, that lovely gentleman nursed me like a mother would her babe, talking to me kindly and wishing me better.

I never knew my father, but if I could have chosen one, it would have been Alfie Watchit. He might have been a criminal but in my eyes he was a saint.

Chapter 7: The South Pacific

I recovered from the lashing well enough, but it took some weeks before I could parade on the deck, and even then my back weren't a pretty sight. Word got out of what Hobbs and his mates had been up to and how I had taken the blame and the punishment without peaching. It made me something of a hero, and showed them in a bad light for seeing a little chap like me beaten to unconsciousness.

For a day or two, I was cock-of-the-walk, strutting around, receiving congratulations and not looking modest about it either. Eventually, Alfie could take my nonsense no longer and delivered me a swipe round the ear that set my ears singing.

'Pack it in, you foolish little beggar,' he said through gritted teeth. 'Have you such a small brain in your head that you have already forgotten what befell you? Think yourself lucky to be alive.'

He made me feel ashamed and ungrateful, I admit it, for had it not been for Alfie nursing and feeding me I would never have survived. I told him I was sorry and he took me in his arms and gave me a great big hug. The first I can remember.

'I have a child,' he said sadly, 'a little younger than you, and what with a twenty year sentence I fear I am too old ever to see him or my wife or brother and sisters again. It's my fault, of course, but now you're all I've got and I don't want to lose you.'

All the tough stuff went out of me at that, and I found myself blubbing into his shirt like a baby.'

'How old are you really?' he asked.

'Twelve,' I said, 'or eleven, perhaps thirteen, it's hard to say when you don't know your birthday. I shouldn't have porked to the beak.'

'Well,' says he, pushing me to arm's length. 'I don't know what lies beyond, but you and I shall make a new life together, look after each other, what do you say?'

'Yes,' I said. 'Like father and son.'

'Like a son,' he said. 'And we shall call today your birthday, if it's alright with you?'

'It's as good as any,' I said.

'Then happy birthday, Jack' he says, 'and many more of 'em'

I won't bother the details of the rest of the journey to Rio and then Cape Town, after which we embarked upon the longest leg of the voyage to

Hobart, in Van Diemen's land, a horrible sounding place where they said there was an animal called the Tasmanian Devil that dragged convicts off and devoured 'em whole. After the things that were done to us, nothing would have surprised me.

Captain Grant never proved anything against Hobbs and company, but nor was he taking chances. After the business with the keys he doubled the guards night and day, which spiked their chances of mutiny even if they had still wanted to.

Not once did we sight land and spotted only the occasional distant ship for the next six thousand miles. Suffice to say, life was just more of what had gone before except that, because of the great distance without putting in to port, food and water were rationed from our first day out of Cape Town. We all grew thinner, convicts and crew alike; many of us being nought but long haired, unshaven skeletons, dressed in filthy rags by the time we reached Hobart.

Despite gnawing hunger, thirst and filth, we grew used to it, the boredom broken only by being forced to witness harsh punishment. The daily routine led us into believing that the voyage would never end, so it came as a shock when the lookout in the crow's nest at the top of the mainmast shouted, 'Land ho! Land to the port bow!'

We rushed excitedly to the rail, and were disappointed to see nothing except the familiar horizon. This, Professor Alfie explained, was because the world was round and the lookout, being much higher than us, could see over the curve. Another marvel. Science, they call it.

Hobart, when we reached it, was a disappointment and little more than a few dull buildings along the coastline with hills behind, looking pretty measly compared with the great cities of Rio and Cape Town.

We stayed only two days, putting off sixty of our number destined for the penal colony at Macquarie Harbour, and taking on fresh food and water. The supply boats brought out considerably less stores than had been loaded at our other stops, leading us to believe that Botany Bay was no great distance compared with that which we had already travelled.

The certainty that our journey was ending cast a cloud over us. As we sailed north for the Australian mainland the activity on deck, which had been busy with men carving, mending, playing instruments, singing and chattering, turned quiet, sullen and gloomy. Unspeaking, our minds were filled with the unknown, as we took turns going to the rail to see what the horizon held.

Chapter 8: New South Wales

A whole day before the lookout spied land, the ship was besieged by flocks of seabirds, the likes of which I had never seen at Deptford or Portsmouth, my only other experiences of the sea, prior to sailing halfway round the world. Amidst laughter, the marines fired their muskets at the swooping, squawking gulls for sport since the birds' flesh was inedible. One or two were downed to great cheers as they plunged into the water. We were so hungry that, never mind what the crew said about the taste, had one crashed to the deck, we would have devoured it feathers, beak and all.

Before we knew it, the officers were shouting orders that sent sailors scrambling into the rigging like monkeys to furl the Lady Eugenia's billowing sails, slowing her progress as she swept past reefs over which foaming, white waves crashed into the dark blue sea. It must have been dangerous because the Captain posted lookouts on all sides to warn of the razor sharp rocks called the Sow and Pigs.

By afternoon, beneath a cloudless sky, our ship had reached the calm waters of what they called the Sydney Heads and for another four hours, we sailed slowly towards our final anchorage in Sydney Cove, passing beautiful bays with silvery, sandy beaches and emerald green islands, giving us hope that we had arrived in paradise. I can tell you honestly, that every man jack of us was desperate to believe that life in this new land would be better than what we had left behind in England. At the sight of it, some even fell to their knees giving thanks to God for bringing us safely to such a wondrous place.

Some of the ships lying at anchor stank to high heaven, so bad that we could smell 'em half a mile off.

'Which country do they come from?' I asked Alfie. 'They ain't flying the Union Jack.' It was a strange flag with red and white stripes and a circle of stars.

'I saw it before in London,' he said. 'They are Yankees, Americans out of Nantucket.'

'Well,' says I, 'I'm glad to be a prisoner of Her Majesty, for those Yankee convicts stink a sight worse than us.'

Alfie laughed. 'The United States does not send convicts to its colonies, since it has none. Only the British government transports criminals to these shores. They are whaling boats, scouring the oceans in search of those great fish we've seen, to kill them and boil their fat into oil. That's what you can smell. Whale oil. It's what keeps the lamps burning across the world. '

'I'd rather put up with our stink than that!'

Alfie stared at the whalers and was quiet for a long time, before saying, 'The United States was a once a British colony until those wise fellows had a revolution and kicked out King George for taxing them too much. They do not like the British Government and I've heard say that American captains don't give a pig's snout for the Queen's Law and welcome escaped convicts aboard as crewmen, without pay. When they reach their home port in Yankeeland they are released, free to go wherever they please.'

I tucked the information away though, after the lashing I'd received, which was still giving me pain, escape was not something I was thinking about.

As we sailed in, what struck me most were the colours. It was another world. London was brown, Portsmouth grey, Tenerife, Rio and Cape Town shimmering blues and greens. Botany Bay was like a diamond sparkling beneath the sun-filled sky, the land yellow, brown and pink, with the lushest vegetation, and flashes of bright colour darting from tree to tree. Birds. Birds so bright that they took my breath away. London's pigeons and sparrows were poor relations of those beauties.

At first sight, it seemed a good place. A beautiful land where nothing could go wrong, where the remaining six and a quarter years of my sentence would fly past and I would find myself on another transport going in the opposite direction, but as a passenger. Then, as I've so often learned to my cost, first sight can be deceptive.

I was looking forward to going ashore but, unbelievably, taking your first steps on dry land after months aboard a rolling ship is the opposite of what you might think, for instead of being able to stand, you roll like a drunken man, legs wobbling, feeling ill. It's the opposite of seasickness. I felt terrible and when I fell to my knees with dizziness, as did others, we were rewarded with blows from the butts of the guards muskets.

We hadn't known what to expect, but it didn't include being pushed on to a bench and having shackles struck on to our ankles all over again. I suppose it was to make sure we didn't jump into the sea and swim the sixteen thousand miles back to Pompey. It was our first inkling that things might not be getting better.

Within minutes of being recorded in a register, our new guards, a scruffy bunch not much different from those in London, began barking orders and we were marched off in a shuffling line, still trying to stand upright after the voyage. Somewhere ahead I saw Hobbs, No Nose, Willis and Springer. I was chained to Alfie in front and, behind, to a poor chap named Birch who had injured his leg during a storm. An open wound was stinking like rotten fish through the filthy rags that were supposed to keep it clean.

We hadn't a clue where we were going and those guarding us were close-mouthed as we passed along streets of houses surrounded by green gardens with neat fences. For those who were not guests of Her Majesty life appeared good, but there were shackled men everywhere in convict uniforms working as gardeners, carpenters and painters.

Alfie whispered over his shoulder, 'I fear that we are no longer convicts, Jack.'

'You could have fooled me,' I said, thinking the old chap had gone off his nut. 'What are we then? Because from the chains around my ankles I can tell I am not a free man. And you neither.'

His next words chilled me to the bone, for I had come to respect his wisdom and truthfulness.

'Slaves,' he said, in a cold voice. 'They have made slaves of us. That is our sole purpose in this forlorn place, to be slaves and serve the rich.'

At the time, I never properly understood what he meant. I'd heard of slavery but that was for Africans, not us loyal subjects of Her Majesty. All I knew was that Alfie feared that a terrible fate had befallen us and, believe me, he was right.

A ragged, chained snake, we marched until nightfall, every step misery as the shackles bit into our skin, chafing down to the bone. Within the hour, my shoes were squelching from my bleeding feet just as if I'd stepped in a puddle of blood. All on empty stomachs and throats as dry as sand.

When a halt was called, we collapsed where we stood and there wasn't a man amongst us with the strength to keep his eyes open.

'We have arrived in hell.' Alfie whispered before I had closed my eyes. 'We must look after each other, Jack, for we have fallen upon testing times.'

During the night, Birch began to wail with pain and thrash around like a lunatic, which was bad for me because we were chained together. The smell of his leg was worse, like a rotting dog on the foreshore at Wapping, and it fair turned my stomach. He was in a dreadful way, bellowing like a bull, shrieking out names and how if we were Christian men we would put him out of his misery. He woke the whole camp, which brought the guards running, none too pleased at being roused from their boozy slumbers.

'Please help him,' said Alfie, as the guards slapped his face and cursed him to be quiet. 'He is very sick.'

'Shut your mouth, or it'll be the worse for you,' said a guard, booting Birch in the ribs.

There was no sympathy from the prisoners who had enough problems, or from the guards who didn't want their sleep disturbed by the wailing of a sick man. As for doctoring, he received none except for having his hands tied behind his back, and his mouth stuffed with rags to gag him. Then a sergeant, an evil looking cove, walloped him behind the ear with a cosh putting him out for the count. It was cruel, I admit, but merciful for at least he could feel no pain.

At daybreak we were kicked awake, given a ration of something that smelled like pond water, a lump of stale bread and a piece of dried meat that was so hard you could've soled your boots with it and walked from Watford to Fagin's place. I couldn't eat the stuff, but tucked it inside my shirt for, sure as eggs were eggs, there would be tougher times ahead.

As for Birch, they chained the miserable soul between two of the biggest chaps who were forced to carry him, or receive a beating themselves. Shackled together we made slow, shuffling progress. How far we walked I cannot tell except that it felt like a hundred miles. Whatever the distance, we were in agony beneath a blazing sun without shade, our heads burning, flies the size of birds feasting on our open wounds.

By late afternoon we reached our destination, a stone-walled compound with wooden gates, inside which was a parade ground surrounded by low buildings with iron barred windows. Bars, I realised upon seeing them, had become as much a part of the furniture of my life as tables and chairs. The unfortunates already in residence never bothered giving us so much as a glance as we slogged by. And why should they? There was nothing special about us, nothing they hadn't seen a hundred times before, and their own misery was every bit as grim as ours. Or worse, and since many of those toiling without shirts exhibited the dreadful signs of the lash on backs criss-crossed with scars, not even Birch's bawling caused a single man to raise his head.

Be thankful for small mercies Fagin used to say before clipping us round the ear.

Unbelievably there was one. And we were thankful for it.

We were marched straight through the gates up to a table where they handed us tin bowls containing a hunk of bread resembling a house brick. Further along, a convict ladled on dollops of warm, brown liquid. If your bowl wasn't underneath it slopped straight on to your feet. One or two weren't quick enough to catch it and there being no second chances, they went hungry, for there was not a man amongst us in the mood for sharing.

Chapter 9: Medicine

I've read the passage in *Oliver Twist* many times, where Mr Dickens writes that while the brave young orphan Oliver was in the workhouse, he dared to ask Mr Bumble, the Parish Beadle, for more gruel. Afterall, the poor boy was hungry. Let me tell you, if he'd tried that in Australia they wouldn't have packed him off to be apprenticed to Sowerberry the undertaker, without first giving him twenty lashes and feeding him bread and water for a month. I never knew the workhouse myself, but from what I gathered from some of the older lags, it was a Mayfair ladies' tea party compared with transportation. There again, credit where credit's due, Mr D told Oliver's story because he had the welfare of the poor at heart and wanted to draw attention to their plight. Children in particular. In my humble opinion, it's a pity that he, or some of the other famous author chums, didn't take up the convicts' cause in their books. That way the horrors of what the government was doing might have ended sooner.

That first night there was quite a kafuffle when Birch started his hellish shrieking all over and the guards, angry at being woken, dragged him off without ceremony.

They were back in no time, chose me and Alfie because we were nearest the door, and led us across the parade ground to the shed lit by oil lamps they called the infirmary. I knew of one in London, St Bart's as I remember, which weren't far from Newgate. I'd once dodged a famous surgeon for his pocket watch, which pleased Fagin so much he gave me an extra sausage with my dinner. But I'd never been inside such a place. I had seen butchers' shops, however, and this looked more like that, with a man they called Surgeon Holmes wearing a brown leather apron, standing behind a table with a nasty array of saws and knives laid out beside him.

Birch, in agony from the pain, was lying on the table, and no sooner had we entered than the Surgeon barked out orders. 'For the sake of this desperate man, do exactly as I say. Do it quickly and do not ask questions.' He pointed to me. 'Sit the little fellow on his chest.'

Without a by-your-leave, his assistants, of which there were two, hoiked me up and flung me across Birch's heaving chest.

'Don't move,' one of them warned me, before stuffing a roll of leather into Birch's mouth to stop him biting off his tongue when he felt the pain of Surgeon Holmes' knife.

They knew their business them chaps

One assistant held the patient's head, while his mate cut the raggy trousers off the damaged leg, Alfie pinning down the other. I'd seen healthier flesh on bodies washed up after a week in the Thames. Then, the Surgeon clamped a diabolical looking device around Birch's shin just below the knee, and twisted a handle until a strap bit deep into the skin, cutting off the blood, by which time the poor man was screaming more from the treatment than his ailment.

'All of you take a strong grip!' shouts Surgeon Holmes, brandishing the knife, which was large enough to chop logs. 'He'll buck like a wild stallion until he passes out.'

As he sliced into the flesh, I closed my eyes and buried my head in Birch's side until he started hollering fit to wake the dead. Just as the Surgeon had said, he bucked so hard that he threw me off and sent me flying across the room to land on the floor.

I wasted no time scrambling to my feet and climbing back on, by which time Birch was out for the count and the Surgeon was attacking the bone with a saw. It was a foul sight but I could not draw my eyes away as the metal teeth carved into the bone, the terrible grating sending shudders through us all. To this day I cannot bear the sound of a carpenter cutting wood.

'The leg is off!' shouted the Surgeon. 'Cloth and tar, quick as you can!'

Much as it terrified me, I continued to watch as the assistant dropped the severed leg to the floor while Surgeon Holmes bound the stump with cloth, slapping on boiling tar between the layers. He loosened the strap around the leg and inspected the stump for bleeding, nodding with satisfaction at his handiwork.

Thanks be that Birch was unconscious, for no man could've stood such treatment whilst awake.

'How long did it take?' asked the surgeon, wiping his hands on a bloody rag and moving away from his patient who lay white as a sheet and looking like a dead man.

'A count of twenty-four, from first cut to last,' replied the assistant standing at Birch's head.

It had seemed longer, but time moves with fearful slowness at times of great strain.

'Not my fastest,' said Surgeon Holmes, 'but quick all the same. Fast is best with amputations.'

He tossed the rag away, looked at me, looked down at my bleeding feet and said, 'Well now, that pair of trotters don't look too good to me. Hop up on that other table, my lad, and we'll deal with them a bit sharpish.'

You can imagine what was going through my brain after witnessing a limb being hacked off and my feet looking not much better than Birch's leg.

Throwing my chest out and voice shaking, I said, 'There's nothing wrong with them. I walked all the way here without as much as a stumble. A bit of mud and dirt, that's all. I ain't bathed in months. When I do, it'll wash off.'

At the surgeon's nod, the larger of the assistants wrapped his arms round me in a bear hug, lifted me on to the table and held me there while they pulled off my tattered shoes and inspected my feet.

'You ain't a-cutting 'em off!' I warned him, raising my fists and jigging a bit like a prize-fighter. 'It'll be the worse for you if you try. They're my feet and I ain't giving you permission to touch 'em.'

'That's a pity,' says he, 'for if you do not let me wash and clean those wounds, you will most likely find yourself in the same position as that desperate soul.' He nodded towards Birch. 'Without 'em, and crawling like a baby.'

I have never breathed a greater sigh of relief, and it was only then that I heard Alfie and the others laughing at my stupidity.

Surgeon Holmes did what he could with what little he had and told me that I should do everything possible to keep the wounds clean, if necessary using some of my drinking water.

'Better to go thirsty than legless,' he said.

Fagin was right about being grateful for small mercies.

I was to meet Surgeon Holmes again in very different circumstances but, at that moment, he was a saint and I shan't forget him in a hurry.

You will have gathered that I was not what you might call a country boy. I had been outside London a few times, not far, but far enough to see an animal or two; pigs, cows, sheep, rabbits and, once, a fox crossed in front of me with a chicken in its mouth. And London was full of horses, mangy dogs and cats a-plenty.

With the exception of the fox, whose only use was to provide sport and entertainment for the pink-jacketed hunting gentry, all those beasts were useful. They either worked for their keep, or were eaten, sometimes both. Even cats, which cannot be trained for tasks and cannot be eaten, did their duty by keeping down the swarms of rats and mice, overrunning the city. You might say that they all fitted in, all played a part in society.

But Australian animals were a different kettle of fish if you'll pardon my mixing of the species.

The kangaroo is an animal the like of which is impossible to imagine until you've seen one bounce past. And bounce they do. I cannot think what God had in mind with such a design. It is a mouse, grey, but as big as man, and it don't run about on all fours, but sits upright balancing on a thick tail, and leaps ten feet at a time using its hind legs. Then, there are the bears. Not the man-sized beasts you see being prodded with a stick and made to dance at English fairgrounds, but little chaps, called koalas, that swing about in the trees all day and chew leaves that make 'em dozy. It's a drug, so they say. The wombat is as big as a boy and lives underground, but most curious of all, is the platypus, a beast made up from the parts of others, with the fur of a beaver, the beak and webbed feet of a duck, and lays eggs you can't eat. There are wild dogs, flea-bitten beasts like on the streets of London, but none as vicious as the dingo what'll drag a babe from its mother's arms and eat it alive. Huge lizards called goannas, snakes whose bite will kill you in a second, poisonous spiders and grasshoppers the size of mice called cicadas are everywhere.

Not one of 'em has got what you might call a proper name, and all of 'em are useless, except for the kangaroo, which we ate whenever we could. In fact, during my time in that strange land, kangaroo grilled over a wood fire was the best meat I tasted.

As for the local people, they ain't white like us, nor black like Africans, but dark brown, looking as if they've been roasted. Since they wear hardly any togs in that blazing sun, they probably have. Dark chaps weren't something new to me, I'd seen 'em before and, as I mentioned, there was an African in Fagin's gang. Up in Mayfair and Belgravia the nobs had house servants from the Queen's territories in the east, Indians, they called 'em, and a lot of Chinamen who lived down Limehouse way on the Thames.

These Australians, or aborigines as they called 'em, were short chaps with mops of wiry hair, not unlike myself, with no possessions whatsoever, not clothes, pots or money, anything, except weapons. Nor did they have proper lodgings, but arranged a few branches into a shelter when it was necessary. They were not farmers, but hunters, living off the land, eating roots and grubs, grasshoppers, birds and any meat they could kill with spears, clubs and boomerangs. Every man amongst them could hurl five spears into the centre of a target before one of Her Majesty's finest could get off a shot and reload, and it was a marvel to watch them throwing the boomerang, a curved wooden blade that killed their prey then flew back into the hand like magic.

A man of my talents would have had slim pickings if he'd had to rely on dodging them for a living. They hadn't learned about stealing, for they left their worldly goods lying where they dropped them for days on end with never a thought that it wouldn't be there when they returned.

Well, what was there to pinch, you might ask?

You would be surprised.

Like I've said so often, where there are men guarding criminals, there's nothing that can't be turned into money, and it were no different in Australia. Soldiers and released convicts going back to England needed cash and would build up a stock of stolen boomerangs and such, which were prized as novelties and fetched good prices on the London markets. The little fellows weren't happy because, without weapons, they couldn't hunt, meaning they went hungry, and that made them angry. They retaliated by killing the white thieves and, in return, the soldiers killed them.

There weren't any love lost between aborigines and soldiers, nor did the poor devils get any better treatment from the convicts, who thrashed them unmercifully for no reason whenever the opportunity arose.

Why is it that no matter how lowly a man is himself, he craves someone lower to despise?

In my experience, it's always them with the least that come off worst, and that was certainly true of the aborigines.

When it came to the treatment of the lowest classes, convicts and aborigines, our masters and the lackeys who kept order for them, treated us with open brutality. I could never look into the eyes of those little men who had lived peacefully in that huge, open country, bothering no one, surviving on what nature provided, without wondering what they thought of the white creatures that had arrived unwanted on their shores to treat them more like dogs than men.

Chapter 10: The Road Camp

We had hardly become used to barracks life with its stiff uniforms covered in black arrows and sleeping three to a bunk, when some of us were picked out and sent to work as an unshackled gang building roads.

Not being chained was a welcome bit of freedom but we still had to work from dawn until dusk smashing rocks with hammers. At night, we ate our one meal of the day round a fire and slept in huts on iron wheels, which we moved with us as the road grew slowly towards the horizon. It seemed to me that if I laboured for the whole of my sentence we would still not reach the end.

Sixty of us lived in three huts, and a curious assortment we were. There were thieves from every corner of England, political prisoners who'd caused trouble in Ireland where they were fighting for independence from the British, and Scots who claimed that the charges against them were trumped because they wanted the English kicked out of their country. None of us mixed with a pair of tricksters who looked and sounded upper class but were rats suspected of being informers. You had to be careful of what you said to everyone except your closest mates, for you never knew who was a nark in the pay of the guards, and peaching was commonplace. Finally, there was a handsome aristocrat, the brother of Lord Posh or some such big wig, who had turned to crime to keep up his expensive tastes after being cut out of his father's will.

The work was hard but without iron weighing us down we could move better, which was a mercy. We were kept at it for months, slogging our guts out under a burning sun, feeling the sting of the whip if we slowed, taking beatings for the amusement of the guards, with nought to eat but rotten pork and hard beans. We rested on the Sabbath and, at night, entertained ourselves telling stories of the ill luck that had brought us to Australia, though there were more than a few who claimed to be innocent of the crime for which he had been transported.

When I told my tale, I was at the point where I had taken Oliver back to Fagin's place, when the aristocrat, Jonathan Radley, pipes up that he knew the old rascal.

'How come?' I asked. 'I cannot believe that the likes of you and he moved in the same circles.'

'I once had some standing in society,' he replied, a curious smile on his face. 'I knew many great houses, and where the owners hid gold and jewellery. In return for a cut of the swag, I tipped off burglars and even drew them plans. It was very profitable. For a while.'

'If you knew Fagin and worked with burglars, then you must have known Bill Sikes,' I said. 'Breaking and entering posh houses was his stock-in-trade.'

'Sikes! Oh, I know him. Never liked the man.' He wrinkled his nose as if a nasty smell had come upon him. 'A cruel devil who treated his dog badly, and his lovely girl worse.'

'Nancy,' I said. 'That was her name. She was kind to us boys. Sikes murdered her before he accidentally topped himself.'

'I am sad to hear it,' he said, 'Not for that blackguard but for that poor girl. He was a bad 'un, alright and cheated me after burgling a house in Wimbledon. He sold the swag to Fagin, forgetting to pay me my share.'

'Fagin's dead,' I said. 'Hanged in public at Newgate. I saw him dangling from the scaffold.'

'I am mightily sorry to hear it,' says Radley, and there were similar mutterings from a others who had also known the old boy. 'He was an out and out villain, but I shall say a prayer for him nevertheless.'

Even in a place like that, the blackest of villains keep their faith.

Radley, it turned out, was a good sort and proved it when Alfie could no longer swing a hammer and collapsed. He was lying helpless while a guard beat him and screamed for him to get up. Radley dropped his own hammer, stepped forward and put a hand on the whip saving Alfie from suffering another blow.

'No need for that,' says he to the guard in a voice that wasn't much more than a whisper. 'Can't you see that the old chap is sick and didn't ought breaking stones. Be a good fellow and let him rest awhile in peace.'

The guard sneered, 'He's a lazy so-and-so who's getting what he deserves,' and was about to take the whip to Radley, when his sergeant came at the trot demanding to know what was going on.

Cool as a cucumber, Radley removed a gold ring from his finger and offered it to the sergeant.

'Get lost,' the sergeant told the guard.

'I'm sure we would work all the better if the old man did the rounds with water to slake our thirst,' Radley said, without a trace of fear in his voice, and eyes as steady as rock.

He pushed the ring a little nearer.

Temptation and greed were written large across the Sergeant's ugly mug. He wiped his brow with a dirty sleeve, snatched the ring and bit it hard, checking that the offering was gold and not bright metal. Satisfied he stuffed it into his pocket.

'You!' he said, kicking Alfie's leg. 'From now on you carry water. And you,' he poked Radley in the chest with his musket, 'take care, for I do not like you or your kind, and I might have to teach you a bit of respect for your betters. Now get back to work.'

As he strode off and we returned to smashing rocks, I said, 'That ring was gold. It could have bought you anything.'

'And it will yet,' he said, with a smile tickling his mouth. 'It belonged to my sister, Elizabeth. She gave it to me on the dock at Portsmouth the day we sailed. Before I leave this place, it will grace my finger again, for that villain only has it on loan.'

The guards were as bored as us convicts. Watching cons break stones in the hot sun is guaranteed to make a man doze off. The Irish, the most rebellious bunch I have ever met in my life, were quick to take advantage and became regular escapers, bolters we called 'em, running in the direction of the Blue Mountains beyond which, it was rumoured, lay China. As the sluggardly guards swung into action, we would rest on our tools and watch the show as they gave chase.

Once, as the guards loosed a hail of musket shot after a character called O'Rourke, Radley had said, 'Good luck to the fellow, I say, but it ain't escaping that's the problem, it's surviving.'

'At least he's free,' I said. 'and though they search they don't bring many back.'

'That doesn't mean they get away,' he said. 'Some are caught by patrols and taken to Sydney for trial and flogging or hanging, and I have heard that a great many more are shot where they're found. But I wouldn't call those who make it to mountains free men. Life is hard living off this land, even for the aborigines, and they're born to it. To run without a plan is to run without hope.'

'And what about them as boards a whaler flying the Yankee flag and sail off free men courtesy of His Majesty the President of United Yankeeland,' I said, as if I were the foreign secretary.

'It is the United States of America,' corrected Radley, as more shots chased O'Rourke further from the camp, 'and the President is not a king but an ordinary man born to parents of no high position.'

'You mean his father weren't a President afore him, not a nob?' My experience was that riches and power were handed on from father to son, not given to the poor.

'His name is Martin Van Buren. His parents were tavern keepers. He had little schooling and educated himself to become a lawyer, then a congressman, which is like a Member of Parliament. Now he is President of the United States of America.'

'I can read,' I said proudly, 'and do letters, Alfie taught me. I could be a lawyer. I'm quite a clever chap really.'

'Well then,' says Radley, 'perhaps one day, if you work hard and turn your back on crime, you might be a president.' He slapped me on the back. 'Remember me when you are rich, Jack.'

Just then, Alfie arrived with drinking water and a tin cup.

'President of where?' he said to Radley.

'The United States,' I said, puffing my chest.

Alfie laughed fit to bust his britches. 'Don't go putting mad ideas into the silly boy's head,' he told Radley. 'He's got to see out his sentence first.'

Radley *had* put an idea in my head and just thinking about a country where an ordinary man could become leader of his people, made me tremble with excitement for, until that moment, I had believed that the whole of my life had been set out for me with no good end in sight.

I never knew it then, but Oliver Twist went to the United States and became a famous lawyer, a rich one too. That's a story for another time, for I did meet him once again in the most unusual circumstances.

The guards paid an aborigine with several bottles of rum to track down O'Rourke and he was brought back after three days with a festering bullet wound in his leg. They didn't bother with a doctor, but strung him up from a tree and made us watch while they stripped every inch of flesh from his back with the cat. He died the following morning and we buried him in a shallow grave near the tree where he'd died.

With the passing months, the road grew longer, though we hadn't a clue where it was going. By my reckoning, what with being on the hulks, the voyage and all that had happened since, I calculated that I must have done at least eighteen months of my time. Some of our mates were luckier than O'Rourke and escaped never to be seen again, more died under the lash and of poisoning from the bites of the deadly snakes and the giant spiders that were everywhere. Others were transferred to jobs on the farms of military officers, government officials and settlers. Assignment, and there was much talk about it. Word was, if you got a good boss, you could see your sentence out quite comfortably. Get a bad 'un, and it was altogether different.

The day was not long coming when it was to be my turn.

Rain had lashed down for a week, the ground was deep puddles and thick mud, and we shivered as we slithered and tried to get a grip on the wet rocks. The guards had taken cover under canvas spread over a bush, not interested in using the whip if it meant getting wet, and happy to see us cold, soaked and struggling. The campfires had been doused and it was set to be another miserable night with cold food in our bellies.

The cart was upon us before we knew it, the sound of its wheels deadened by the pounding rain. A fat corporal sat on the driver's bench, two guards and four prisoners crouching in the back. All were drenched to the skin and I was surprised to see that these were my old shipmates from the Lady Eugenia; Hobbs, No Nose, Springer and

Willis, all looking like drowned rats. I can honestly say I was none too happy to remake their acquaintance.

We were lined up and, after close inspection of a list upon which the ink was running in black streams, the corporal picked out me, Alfie, Radley and two Irishmen to go with them.

While they were striking shackles on to our legs, our Sergeant paraded up and down saying his farewells.

'You scum will miss me,' he mocked. 'You'll miss my tender touch and how I've been like a mother, looking after you like babes in arms.'

He stopped directly in front of me, slapped my head, sniffed and spat into a puddle.

'I never liked you. You're a bad 'un to my way of thinking, and good riddance, I say.'

I've never been able to keep my trap shut, especially to authority, and it usually ends up the worse for me, but there was an opportunity not to be missed and I heard myself saying, all sarcastic, 'Thank you, sir, I will miss your kindness.'

With that, he grabbed my shirt and dragged me towards him, silly fellow, for if he had any brains in his skull he would have known the folly of getting too close to the Artful Dodger.

'Don't ever let me see your horrible face again,' he snarled. 'For if our paths should happen to cross, it won't be no picnic for you.'

I looked upset, hung my head and said, 'Sorry, Sergeant, I will try to live a better life in future.'

The corporal and guards were close-mouthed and wouldn't let on where they were taking us or why, but even in that pouring rain, with thunder and lightning crashing over the Blue Mountains, we were pleased not to be smashing rocks.

Eventually the sun showed himself, we dried out and jogging along on that rickety, uncomfortable cart began to feel like a bevy of princes on our way to the Royal Enclosure at Ascot Races.

It was Alfie who started singing, and we sang every song we knew at the tops of our voices, Hobbs and pals joining in with gusto. The kangaroos, wombats and aborigines must have thought us ridiculous. Then I noticed a tinge of sadness on Radley's face.

'What's up,' I said. 'Ain't you glad to be away from such hard labour?'

'Without doubt,' he said, 'but it happened so quickly that I was unable to retrieve Elizabeth's ring. It was a great comfort to me, and I cannot bear the thought of it being in the possession of that foul oaf.'

The rain was streaming down his face but I could still see that there were tears on his cheeks.

'Well,' I says, holding out my hand towards him, 'perhaps it'll turn up one day. You never know with these things. Afterall, you said it was only a loan.'

I shall never forget the look on his face when I opened my fist and he caught sight of his sister's ring on my little finger. His jaw dropped and his eyes widened so far that I feared they would pop from his head.

'But, Jack, how the devil…?' He snatched up my hand, staring at it in utter disbelief.

'Trade secret,' I said, tapping my nose. 'And a half sovereign to go with it.'

I opened my hand to reveal a gold coin that had lain in the Sergeant's pocket alongside Elizabeth's ring.

Fagin hadn't named me Artful Dodger for nothing.

Chapter 11: Good Hope Plantation

When Alfie had told me on the day we landed that he feared we were slaves, I hadn't understood what he meant. We were prisoners of Her Majesty, being punished for our crimes. If we kept our noses clean and did our time, we would be set free. From what I knew, slaves were black, Africans or maybe even aborigines, who were bought and sold in markets like cows and sheep, without a hope of going free. Radley said that many people in the United States owned slaves, which considering an ordinary man could become President, or a British prisoner could become free by boarding a Yankee whaler, was quite a puzzle to me.

We were Englishmen. I had heard sailors in Portsmouth and on the Lady Eugenia sing, *Britons, never, never, never shall be slaves.* Alfie was wrong.

I soon realised what he meant when, after three days hard travelling with hardly any grub, the cart forked on to a track where a signpost pointed us towards Good Hope Plantation.

The land was well kept with cattle, sheep and fields of crops. It weren't like a great farm in England but you could smell money all the same. There were workers here and there, all wearing prison garb, though marked differently to ours.

It was two hours more, with the shadows lengthening, before we reached the big house, where the owner, Mr Arthur McIntyre, and his overseer, Matthew Grimshaw, were waiting for us. They were well-dressed and clean but brutish looking, and it was no comfort that Grimshaw, a scrawny man with a nose more hooked than Fagin's, was slapping a riding crop against a polished boot.

'Get them out and line them up!' he bawled, in a voice bigger than himself.

We needed no further bidding to stand up and stretch our numb legs, though it didn't stop the idiot guards putting on a fine show of power by whacking us with their musket butts and kicking us off the cart. I ended up sprawling in the dust and being dragged to my feet by the collar.

'It don't look like they've got much work in 'em, Mr Grimshaw,' sneered McIntyre. 'I told the Governor I wanted only prime workers but I doubt we shall get much from these.'

He was hardly a top-notch specimen himself what with a roll of stomach hanging over his belt, red jowls and a nose full of purple veins from swilling too much port and brandy. Dressed in rags and pitched on to the streets of Shoreditch, you wouldn't have been able to tell him from the rest of us oiks.

'I fear you're right, Mr McIntyre, sir,' replied the overseer. 'They shall have to be knocked into shape, and I'm the very man to do it.'

McIntyre said, 'Tell 'em their rights, Mr Grimshaw,' and turned towards the house. He hesitated then, as if remembering something, crossed to our ragged line and stared closely into Alfie's face without saying a word. It was downright creepy. 'Have 'em up and ready at sunrise,' he called over his shoulder as he walked off.

Grimshaw inspected each of us in turn. Arriving at Alfie, he put the crop under the old boy's chin, forcing his head back.

'You cost Mr McIntyre a fortune, did you know that?'

'I have never set eyes on him in my life,' said Alfie, all of a tremble.

'Nor he you,' said Grimshaw, 'but your name is well known to him. He read it in the newspapers. They take a few months to get here, but it's still news to us. You almost ruined his family when he bought the government bonds you'd been forging. When he saw in The Times that you had been transported to New South Wales, he spoke to the Governor personally about making you his special guest here at Good Hope.' He chuckled nastily. 'He wants repayment, and I shall see that he gets it, every penny.'

Alfie went as white as a sheet. 'I am a hard-worker, sir, and will not shirk my duties, you can be sure of it.'

'You will not,' barked Grimshaw. 'Nor the rest of you.' The crop whistled through the air as he strode off a few paces then swung round to face us. 'You are prisoners of the State, assigned to Mr McIntyre as servants of this plantation with no rights other than those the government grants by law. To be fed, housed and given a bed. You are required to obey all lawful commands. Failure to do so will result in your going before a magistrate for trial and punishment. You will work from sun up to sun down resting on Sundays and Christmas Day. Do not attempt to escape. You can run, but you cannot hide and all attempts will result in your being sent for trial and, likely as not, hanged for your trouble.' On that happy note, he walked off, shouting, 'Follow me, you filthy lot! Your shackles will be struck off, you will be fed and receive new uniforms. In the morning you will start work.'

As we shuffled after him, Alfie came close and whispered. 'You would do well to steer clear of me from now on, Jack, for I am as good as dead, and they will not rest until they have put me six feet under.'

'They cannot murder you,' I said. 'You are a prisoner, it would be a crime.'

He laughed. 'Whatever they do they will make it legal, have no doubts about that. In any case, who cares about whether an old forger lives or dies.'

I turned to Radley. 'Did you hear what he said?'

'Plainly enough,' he replied, 'and if McIntyre did suffer such losses from Alfie's handiwork, then I fear the old chap is a marked man.'

'And they call this place Good Hope,' I said.

'For me No Hope is more like it,' said Alfie. 'How I escaped the hangman's noose I shall never know, but I am here for twenty years. Plenty of time for them to do their worst, even after you and Jonathan are long gone.'

Radley took his arm in a firm grip. 'Do not say such things, I beg you. If we stick together we will come through this.'

That night, we ate hot porridge and slept in hard bunks with thin blankets. We breakfasted on cold porridge, washing it down with a mug of weak beer. After the roads, it was like luncheon at the Savoy Hotel. We received stiff new boots and uniforms, the first clothes I'd worn in my life that hadn't first been on the back another before me, dead or alive. The boots hurt worse than walking barefoot on city cobbles and the uniforms cut into every joint and itched worse than a trouserful of red ants.

Grimshaw and his foreman put No Nose and his mates from the Lady Eugenia to work with a gang building a bridge that would shorten the journey to the main road. The Irish became shepherds on account of having worked with sheep. At least, that's what they told Grimshaw when he asked if they had a trade, but those boys could spin a good tale and there wasn't an ounce of truth in it. Alfie was dispatched to the kitchen garden and Radley, who knew something of horses, though more as a betting man at Epsom Downs than as a groom, was sent to the stables. I was made handyman, and I had not the faintest idea what it meant.

It didn't take long to discover that there were quite a bunch of prisoners at Good Hope, women amongst 'em, not only on the land, but in the house where they cooked, washed, cleaned and waited at table. In the dairy the cons made butter and cheese, there was a bakery, brewery, pickling shed and a butchery where meat was smoked and preserved. The best produce went first to feeding the family, then for sale in Sydney markets and the leftovers to feed us cons. Overseer and foremen apart, nobody was earning wages, meaning that Mr McIntyre and family were making themselves rich on the backs of others, more proof that where there's criminals, there's money to be made. Still, it wasn't such a bad a trade when you think about it. We had done wrong and it was better than serving time banged up in Newgate or breaking rocks.

There were aborigine families on the plantation. Not the way I'd seen 'em in the bush but living in ratty huts called the village that you could smell before you saw it. Anywhere else it would have been called a slum, and it ponged worse than Limehouse in August. The settlers had taken their land and the poor blighters had been cut off from everything they knew, whereas we cons had been transported to the other side of the world, to a life more or less like England. Somehow, none of it seemed right. Without being able to hunt, men, women and children spent their days sitting in the dust smoking bad tobacco and drinking rum that made 'em angry at best and drove 'em mad at worse. Alfie told me they never had diseases until the settlers got there and even catching a cold from a foreigner could kill 'em stone dead. They were an unhappy bunch, led by a headman who wore a leather thong around his neck, from which hung a copper plate engraved with the word *chief*.

A chief in charge of nothing.

They had no idea of work as we Englishmen knew it, having never had to earn money to buy food, and were kept by McIntyre for tracking stray animals and escaping convicts, for which they received handouts of food and alcohol.

All up, they were a desperate lot, not that anyone wanted to help as they were considered little more than animals.

I'm no philosopher now, and I weren't then but uneducated as I was, I could see the wrong of it.

To start my new job, Grimshaw walked me round behind the stables to a newly built workshop. Sitting in the dust outside was an aborigine boy of about my age.

'Get out of it!' bawled Grimshaw, delivering a stinging clout to the boy's ear and kicking his backside. 'Be off, you thieving pest before I trounce you good and proper.'

A carpenter looked up from his work.

'This 'ere's John Dawkins, who will assist you,' announced Grimshaw. 'He's a thief, so watch where you're leaving those precious tools of yours.'

'Thank you, Mr Grimshaw. Welcome to my workshop, Mr Dawkins,' he said, in the soft way of those who come from the west of England and ain't as sharp-witted as us London boys. He was youngish, in his twenties, with a large head and a smile as wide as a rainbow. He wiped his hands on a leather apron and stretched one towards me. 'I am Henry Wilkes and right glad to have your company and your help, for there is much to keep in good order.'

I looked around. 'I know nought of working with wood,' I said, 'and have no training with tools.'

'Then it is your lucky day,' says he, 'for you have fallen in with a time-served carpenter who will teach you a trade, if you are willing.'

There had been a time when the only work I knew was thievery. True, it needs special skills, and it ain't hard sweat like breaking rocks twelve hours a day but there's no future in it either. Being apprenticed in England was a costly business, parents having to pay a master for seven years. I ask you, who could afford to pay to work for others? Families were so poor that they wanted money coming in, not going out. It didn't make sense. For the likes of us, learning a trade was beyond imagination. Now, sixteen thousand miles away from what passed for home I was being offered just that. Sometimes life is upside down.

I could hear Fagin laughing, 'Dodger, my dear, such work is not for a man of your intelligence, with fingers as nifty as any artist.'

And where had my previous trade got me? Seven years transportation and a back striped with scars after tasting the cat aboard the Lady Eugenia.

There again, what had an honest trade done for carpenter Henry Wilkes? You'd not be far wrong for thinking he was no better off than me.

'I am willing to learn,' I said. 'For in five and a half years I shall be free and looking to earn wages, p'raps to pay for an education and become a lawyer, like Mr Martin Van Buren.'

'Who?' said Henry.

'The President of the United States,' I informed him all scholarly. 'Nobody calls me Mr Dawkins, it's Jack to you.'

'Then, Jack, you shall be gone from this place long before me,' he says. 'I am a lifer and shall never see England again. My only hope is that if I can please Mr McIntyre and stay out of trouble, I shall be granted a ticket-of-leave to earn my living here in Australia.' 'Well,' I says, 'if you're doing life, you must have done a sight worse than me, who is a pickpocket by trade. What did you do, rob the Bank of England?'

'Oh, I was not condemned as a thief,' he replied. 'In that respect I can claim to be as honest as the day is long. I was sentenced for murder.'

That shocked me, I can tell you, and a moment went by in which I went quite quiet. It seems it is a habit of mine to fall in with wrong 'uns.

Taking a step away from him, I said, 'And they never strung you up? They strung up Fagin and he was nought but a fence.'

'Fagin? Fence?'

'My old employer,' I said as if Fagin had been a respectable banker. 'They hanged him at Newgate for receiving stolen goods. It's called fencing in criminal lingo. But it ain't murder!'

He laughed. 'Enough! You have nothing to fear from me. Pick up that plank and that bag of tools and follow me before Mr Grimshaw decides we are lazy. It is best to keep a clean record. You may address me as Henry. And he...' he pointed to the door where the aborigine boy was sitting in the dust staring at us, '...is called Dungara!'

'Dungara,' I said. 'A queer name I must say.'

'I have learned a little of their language,' said Henry. 'It means lightning. He can run fast and tracks lost animals and escaping convicts. When he has nothing to do, he watches me. At first it was strange, but now I am used to it.'

I waved to Dungara who did not wave back.

I was not properly apprenticed to Henry but, murderer or not, he was kind and a fine teacher who patiently showed me how to use hammer, chisel and saw. The first time he asked me to cut timber I couldn't, and ran out of the workshop all of a sweat. It had reminded me of Birch. Henry wasn't having any nonsense and forced me to finish but, to this day, I avoid such work if I can.

Some days we toiled in the workshop, on others we did jobs in the stables and garden and inside the house, repairing doors and windows. Proper, regular work, even if unpaid, was new to me and I was always happy to get out of my bunk and into the workshop. The same went for most of the others who, despite moaning and groaning, would not have swopped for the roads.

But not for Alfie.

True to Grimshaw's words, McIntyre was paying him out by treating him bad, but always with a clever eye to observing the law because us assigned men had certain rights. The old chap was forbidden to eat and sleep with us and forced to make do with scraps, curled up in a shed where they kept the gardening tools. He could hardly stretch out and had not even been given anything to cover himself with at night, until Radley discovered his plight and risked punishment by slipping him a horse blanket. It was tattered but would keep him warm. We were under strictest orders not to speak with him.

We were repairing a greenhouse, and Alfie was on his knees a few feet away planting out seedlings, when he started to cough.

'Are you alright?' I whispered. 'You don't sound too good to me.'

He shooed me away. 'I am alright, Jack.' He coughed and spat into the flowerbed. There was a gob of dark blood in it. 'Do not be caught breaking their rules by talking to me or it will be the worse for you.'

I kept an eye on him for the rest of the day, but he weren't any better by the time we packed our tools and left.

Radley's face blackened with rage when I took him aside after supper and told him. 'There was blood when he spat,' I said.

'They will kill him for certain,' he said. 'That's what the devil McIntyre is after.'

'He has nought to eat save crusts and water,' I said. 'He daren't take a carrot or an apple for fear they will call it stealing and beat him. The dogs are better fed, and he has bruises, though Grimshaw never hits him in view of others. We must do something before it is too late for the old chap.'

Chapter 12: The Truth about Oliver Twist

Good Hope did not receive many visitors, and those who came usually arrived on horseback or by light carriage, so there was great excitement when six canvas covered, heavy wagons each drawn by a pair of bullocks, creaked, groaned and swayed slowly down the dirt road towards the house. You'd have been forgiven for thinking that we were watching a coronation procession to Westminster Abbey, the way the lags stopped work to admire the caravan. Even the aborigines squatted at the roadside astonished by the sight of such massive animals.

Henry and me were working in the library building bookshelves, and went to peer at the spectacle through the open window. Dungara was crouching outside. I was about to shout at him, but Henry stopped me.

'Leave the lad be, Jack,' he said. 'He does you no harm and would like to help, 'cept our bosses will not allow him.'

'He stares so,' I said. 'It unnerves me.'

Henry pointed to the wagons. 'I heard that a fast ship from England docked in Sydney two weeks ago,' he said. 'There will be new books to put on these shelves.'

That night the drivers tethered the bullocks and slept in the open, forbidden to associate with us. The following morning, with the heavy lifting being done by convicts, unloading began. Furniture and carpets, bolts of fabric and cloth, and dozens of boxes and trunks full of the latest clothes were carried in and directed to rooms by Mr McIntyre, who strutted around waving a sheaf of papers. Five packing cases, a sweating man on the corner of each, were brought into the library and placed near a long table, which had been covered in layers of felt by the servants.

'Open them carefully, carpenter,' Grimshaw told Henry, 'and you, young thief, set each book on the table spine uppermost so that the title can be read. I shall send a man to check them against the ship's manifest.'

Before I could hold back, I heard my big mouth saying, 'Sir, I beg your pardon, but I am able to read. I can do it if you wish.'

At that Grimshaw swung round faster than if he'd been bitten on the backside by an angry dingo. 'What did you say, thief? Read? You?'

Stupidly, as was often my way, I had ignored the cons first rule, never volunteer. And the second, never give information.

'I thought it would be helpful, sir,' I said, casting my eyes down and wishing I'd kept quiet.

Grimshaw grabbed me by the neck.

'Liar! How does a rotten villain like you know how to read?' he snarled, stinking breath burning my face. 'You never went to school.'

Well, I had, Fagin's Academy for Young Pickpockets, where I was top student but, wisely, I thought better of mentioning it.

'It is a long voyage from England,' I said, all of a tremble. 'I learned on the ship.'

His piggy eyes narrowed. 'Who would want to teach scum like you?'

'One of the lags,' I said. 'We were mates, he gave me a Bible and taught me. I read it many times, every day in fact. I still have it.'

'Bible!' He ground his teeth. 'The likes of you has no right reading the Holy Book!' He tightened his hold until I gasped for breath. 'I'll give you Bible!'

I was sure he was about to backhand me, when I was saved by McIntyre's voice.

'Leave him be, Mr Grimshaw.'

Grimshaw let go instantly.

'He is a lying thief, Mr McIntyre, sir, claiming he can read, if you've ever heard such a thing in your life. He has a motive, that's for sure.'

'I heard,' said McIntyre. 'The world would be a safer place if every felon read the Good Book.' He selected a volume from the table, opened it without looking and thrust it at me.

'Read.'

I took it and stared at the lines, saying silent thanks that the words were small and thanking Alfie for making me practice even when I complained. I cleared my throat, and spoke.

'*I – stood – tip-toe – upon – a – little – hill,*' I began slowly to be certain that every word was correct. '*The – air – was – cooling – and – so – very – still…*'

'So, you can read,' said McIntyre, removing the book from my shaking hands and inspecting the cover, running a finger along the author's name embossed in gold letters. 'John Keats. Never read him myself, I'm not a poetry lover like my wife and daughters. Too sentimental. This person who taught you,' he hesitated, never taking his eyes off mine for a moment, 'is he here, at Good Hope?'

I wished the floor would open up and swallow me, for the last person I wanted to mention was Alfie, considering he was having a bad enough time without me making matters worse.

'I don't remember his name,' I said. 'He was just a lag they put off in Hobart.'

'Look at his face,' cried Grimshaw. 'He's lying. The young thief is a bare faced liar.'

McIntyre appeared not to hear him. 'From the Governor's papers, there are only two who might possibly be able to read. The man Radley and the forger, Watchit. Since Radley arrived on these shores a full year before you, it cannot have been him, which leaves only one other.'

I said nothing.

Grimshaw said, 'Shall I thrash the truth out of him, Mr McIntyre, sir?'

McIntyre ignored the overseer who was hopping from foot to foot, red-faced and more than ready to take his riding crop to my hide.

'Take care Jack Dawkins,' he said in a low voice, 'for I am not a man to be trifled with. Come Mr Grimshaw, there are still three wagons to be unloaded afore nightfall.' He tossed the book of poetry on to the table.

I gave it a minute after they had gone, before whispering, 'I don't understand Grimshaw's anger. I was only trying to be useful.'

Henry smiled. 'He wears fine clothes, earns wages and has power over your every move,' he replied. 'But you can do something he cannot. Read. He does not like it, because it gives you knowledge that he does not have.'

Truth to tell, it seemed absurd. 'I should've known better and kept my trap shut. Will it be the worse for me? For Alfie?'

'Who knows,' said Henry, 'but you can be certain we shall find out soon enough.'

The following morning, we had no sooner set about our task than McIntyre arrived with Grimshaw and handed me a sheaf of papers.

'Here is a list of books ordered in London which should now be packed in these cases,' he said. 'You will find each volume and make a mark to confirm it is here.'

I took the papers. 'Yes, sir.'

'Wash your hands and wear these when you are touching the covers. The books are valuable and I do not want them damaged.' He handed me a pair of white cotton gloves.

With his departure, I began work, carefully ticking off books as I found them. Quite interesting it was, too, and although I was curious as to their contents, I was afraid to look inside, except for one, a book of maps and, across two pages, Australia. I could see Sydney, the rivers and the coast, all the small towns and harbours, though I could not tell distances. In the same box were dozens of rolled charts, a compass and sextant much the same as those used on the Lady Eugenia by Captain Grant.

'Look, Henry, maps,' I said, unfurling a roll. 'An escaper would find them very useful.'

Henry became nervous. He was a mild man who slept in the back of the workshop and kept himself to himself so as not to endanger his prospects of receiving a ticket-of-leave.

'Be quiet, Jack,' he begged, holding a finger to his lips. 'Talk of escaping is dangerous and can see a man brought before a magistrate and punished. Roll it up, before someone sees.'

Seeing how he was quite agitated, I immediately set the map aside and picked up a red, leather-bound volume. The title was *The Pickwick Papers* and its author, can you believe it, Charles Dickens. It was the first time I had heard Mr D's name and there was a picture of him in the front. Quite a handsome chap he was, who would have made fine pickings in the West End.

I ticked it off, put it on the table and picked up next, which looked exactly like its twin in the same matching binding.

You could have knocked me down with a feather.

My stomach went queasy. I wanted to be sick.

On the spine, it said *Oliver Twist*.

I couldn't move.

You have to admit that it is a most unusual name and I have never heard of another person with that monniker before or since, and I doubt there is another in the world.

A bit frightened, I turned the cover to face me.

There was no mistaking it.

In even bigger letters, as if shouting at me, it said *Oliver Twist*.

Carefully, I opened the cover and one by one, turned the pages, not reading but looking at the pictures drawn by Mr. George Cruickshank. Underneath the first was written *Oliver escapes being bound apprentice to the sweep*. It meant nothing to me because, at that time, I didn't know his story. Beneath the next, it said, *Olivier is introduced to the respectable old gentleman*.

I dropped the book in fright, and froze like a statue. Was that not what I had done using the exact words, *respectable old gentleman*, to lure Oliver back to Fagin's place?

'Take care,' says Henry, as it crashed to the floor. 'You heard Mr McIntyre say that they are valuable and you don't want to be in trouble for damaging 'em.'

'Sorry,' I said, frozen to the spot.

'Well, get on with it,' he says. 'Pick it up before Grimshaw catches you a-slackin'.'

'Right,' I said, reaching for the book.

I opened it again and stared at the picture.

A bearded man with a hooked nose and a Jew's skullcap, stood in front of a fireplace, toasting fork in his hand. Without the shadow of a doubt, it was Fagin, and he was wearing the very same coat as when I'd seen him swinging on Newgate gallows. Next to him, was a short, ugly cove with a piggy nose, wearing an oversize tailcoat and a top hat tilted rakishly on his head. Dressed like that, it could only have been me. Around a table, boys were smoking clay pipes, and in front of us all, the thin lad doffing his cap to Fagin was none other than dear Oliver Twist.

Words on the opposite page jumped out at me, and I read them silently, lips trembling.

"This is him, Fagin," said Jack Dawkins, "my friend Oliver Twist."

To this day, it is a mystery to me why Mr Dickens chose Oliver Twist as his hero when there were thousands of others in the same plight.

At that moment, the picture and my name in black and white brought back meeting Oliver on the Watford road. He was worn out and half-starved. I thought I was doing him a kindness taking him back to Fagin's place. Who could ever have imagined how it was going to work out?

The old rogue had kept him inside for weeks, picking embroidered initials out of kerchiefs, cleaning wallets, and polishing the scratches off pocket watches. All the while, that innocent boy had not a clue where these things had come from.

Becoming bored and lacking fresh air, he had begged Fagin to allow him out. His wish was granted, in the charge of Charley Bates and me. Pick-pocketing is a dangerous game, especially since Sir Robert organised his Peelers and we weren't none too happy about it but there weren't no going against Fagin.'

'Take good care of him, Dodger,' Fagin had warned as we left for work. 'Teach him well and don't let him come to any harm. And make sure there's plenty of swag to pay for your supper.'

'How will we pay Mr Fagin?' I remember Oliver asking. 'Will we be earning money?'

Charley laughed and I said, 'Something like that, young Oliver.'

The three of us sauntered around for a while making mischief here and there, and pinching breakfast off a fruit stall. We were emerging into Camberwell Green, when I spotted a posh gent wearing a bottle-green coat and white trousers, carrying a bamboo cane. He was at a bookstall and I could smell money.

'See him?' I asked the others.

'Yes, I see him,' replied Oliver, without an idea in his empty head of what was about to happen.

'An easy mark,' says Charley, rubbing his hands. 'Take note, Oliver, for this is how to do it.'

Without further ado, we set off across the square with Oliver trotting a few paces behind like a lost puppy. He never had a clue in his innocent head as to what we were about.

There being no sign of Peelers, I wasted no time slipping my hand into the gent's pocket and withdrawing a handsome silk kerchief, which I passed to Charley. I was about to lift his wallet when I caught sight of Oliver staring wide-eyed. Fearful that the silly boy would say something and rumble us, we took off at high speed, signalling him to do likewise. For a moment, he stood frozen to the spot, realising where all those kerchiefs, wallets, watches and jewellery had come from.

When he began to run, the old gent saw him, rummaged in his pockets and, missing the kerchief, shouted, 'Stop thief!'

Rounding the first corner, Charley and me pulled a dodge by leaning in a doorway, stuffing clay pipes into our mouths and acting like a couple of old codgers who'd been standing there for hours. When Oliver came running past with the crowd in hot pursuit, we joined the chase until a fellow with fists the size of hams brought him down with a blow that would have felled a champion prize fighter. The poor boy lay there on the cobbles out for the count.

'Where is the gentleman who was robbed?' someone called as the crowd surrounded his unconscious body.

'Here he is,' says another, making way for the old gent to come the fore.

'Is this the boy, sir?'

The old gent pushed into the circle of honest citizens who had prevented Oliver's escape. 'Yes,' he said, 'I am afraid that it is.'

'Afraid!' murmured the crowd. 'That's a good 'un! They should hang him straight off.'

'Poor little fellow,' said the old gent, ignoring them. 'He has hurt himself.'

'I did that,' said the man who had knocked him down. 'I cut my knuckle on his mouth, stopping him. Is there a reward, sir?'

Charley and me had seen it all before and needed no telling which way the wind was blowing. With a quick glance at each other, we put our hands in our pockets and whistling all nonchalant-like, left the scene before young Twist could finger us for accomplices.

We were quaking with fear when we got back, because we new Fagin's temper.

'Where is the boy?' had been his first question. 'Where is Oliver?' His villain's nose told him that something was wrong and he swung his toasting fork from one to another. 'Speak up, or I swear I'll throttle the pair of you.'

'The Peelers have him,' I said. 'I expect they've taken him to the magistrate on Mutton Hill.'

Hearing this, Fagin had flown into a rage and taken a swipe at me with the fork, which I ducked but not before it had whipped off my hat. He was in a dreadful tizz, fearing that Oliver would identify him to the law. He stamped about, threatening to break our skulls and cut our throats, until he got up a plan whereby Nancy would go down to Mutton Hill pretending to be searching for her lost little brother, and find out what had happened to him.

I accompanied her, and what a fine actress she was, bawling her eyes out, tearing her hair and stamping, until the gaoler told her that Oliver had given his name as Tom White and had not peached. Mr Fang, the magistrate, had wanted to sentence him to three months in gaol but reluctantly released him when a witness gave evidence that another boy had done the dipping. Fang had no option but to allow him to leave in the care of the old gent, Mr Brownlow, who had taken pity on him.

I felt myself sweating remembering that day.

'Jack!' Henry's voice seemed far off. 'Jack! What is going on? You've been staring at that book for ages.'

I still could not take my eyes off it. 'Sorry,' I said. 'I was thinking.'

'Well, stop at once and get working,' he said, 'before you land us both in trouble.'

He knelt down and returned to the hole he was drilling in a length of timber. He could not see me, and a quick look around showed there was no one at the door. In a flash, I lifted my jacket, stuffed *Oliver Twist* into my trousers, and picked up another book from the table.

My heart sank when, out of the corner of my eye, I saw Dungara peering in through the open window, staring in that strange way of his. The blighter had seen everything.

When I took a step towards him, he disappeared into the shrubbery faster than a rabbit what's spotted a gamekeeper. My mind was troubled for the rest of the day, at the end of which McIntyre and Grimshaw arrived to inspect our progress. McIntyre praised Henry on the craftsmanship that had gone into fitting the shelves, before taking the list from the table and running a finger down the ticks next to the titles.

'I see one is missing,' he said. '*Oliver Twist* by Charles Dickens does not appear to be here.'

My throat was as dry as brick dust, the book burning my stomach. I had to think quick.

'I have not yet found it, sir. They are not packed in order but according to size to fit as many into the boxes as possible. I may yet come across it.'

He did not appear overly concerned.

'I hope so,' he said. 'I see that we also have Mr Dickens' *Pickwick Papers*. I read it in its original form last year. It was published in monthly parts. Quite excellent. I understand this new one, *Oliver Twist*, shines a light on the plight of London's poor and the exploitation of children by criminals.'

A fat lot you know or care about them, I thought, but had the wit to keep my mouth firmly shut. I was learning, you see.

Grimshaw, who was not one for pleasantries with criminals, and had a bloodhound's nose when it came to sniffing out jiggery-pokery, said, 'He's not even finished one box, Mr McIntyre. At this rate, he'll be another week or more. He needs a sharp lesson, I'd say.'

'There's no particular hurry,' says McIntyre. 'I would prefer to see the work done properly. Besides, the shelves are not ready. It will be ten days before they have been French polished and are ready to receive books. Hopefully, by then I shall have returned from my business in Sydney.'

I had to read *Oliver Twist* to know what it said.

If I played it clever, it would be at least a week before I needed to finish the checking and, if I was careful, I could hang on to it until then, reading by night.

Chapter 13: Things go wrong

We cons did not go hungry. Left to Grimshaw we would have been on a diet of bread and water but McIntyre, for all his bad ways, wanted hard work from his convicts and understood that they laboured best with full bellies. The grub weren't exactly up to the standards of a Pall Mall hotel but there was plenty of it and always piping hot. When they learned of Alfie's predicament, each man willingly gave up a portion of his supper to make sure he was well fed. Even Hobbs and company chipped in without complaining.

'If anyone is caught, McIntyre will punish the lot of us,' said one of the Irish we called Paddy. 'It's a dangerous game.'

'He won't want the whole of his workforce lying abed with bleeding backs,' said another. 'So, who's doing it? Who'll be Alfie's waiter?'

There weren't many takers for the task until Radley spoke. 'Tonight after dark I shall take the food to the old chap. But someone must keep their eyes peeled. As our good friend Paddy says, it is not wise to be caught defying that blackguard.'

'I have a better idea,' I said. 'Let me take it. I am smaller than you and can cross the garden unseen.' I had other business with Alfie but I weren't letting on just then.

'As you wish,' said Radley, 'but take care. McIntyre might not flog us all, but he would see the carrier lashed as an example to the rest.'

'I need candlelight,' I said, taking Radley aside. 'Can you oblige?'

'I won't ask why,' he said. 'There are stubs collected from the house. I shall fetch some.'

After dark, a canvas bag looped about me, I snuck off, keeping to the shadows of the garden wall, crawling under a hedge, wriggling through the vegetables. It reminded me of going a-burgling with Sikes and his mates. When I came to Alfie's shed I put my mouth close to the door, tapped and whispered, 'Alfie, open up!'

'Who is it?'

'Jack! Quick. Open the door.'

After some scuffling, it opened and I slithered in on my belly like a snake. There were no windows and it was blacker than outside. I felt around, until my hand came to rest on Alfie's leg.

'I have food from your mates in the barracks.'

'You have put yourself in danger, Jack. And the rest of the boys, for if Grimshaw hears of this…'

'Well I shan't tell 'im if you promise the same,' I interrupted, not wishing to hear any more warnings of floggings. I took out a candle stub and tinderbox, and struck iron against flint. When it flared, I touched the wick and, in the flickering light, pushed the bag towards him. 'Eat!' I whispered.

Fair play to them lags, they did not palm him off with scraps but proper cuts of meat, every bit as good as those they had eaten themselves.

Alfie wolfed it down, he belching loudly enough to wake them up in the main house, and said, 'I shall keep the rest for the morrow,'

'There will be food every day from now on,' I told him. 'Eat your fill.'

'You boys are good to me. Say thank you from an old man.'

'I will,' I said. 'Alfie, I need your help.'

'I am hardly in a position to help anyone,' he chuckled, 'locked up like a dog in a kennel.'

'Yes you can,' I said, removing *Oliver Twist* from inside my clothing. 'You can read this to me.'

'You are able to read very well,' he said, puzzled. 'Or have you forgotten all I taught you?'

'I have not,' I said. 'I practice when I can, which ain't often, but this book has many big words and is not like the Bible. You also read quicker than me. Please, Alfie, help me.'

'Where did you get it?'

When I told him that I had pinched it he was angry, said he wouldn't read it, nor should I, and that it was best returned before I was discovered and punished.

'Please,' I begged, 'it means a lot to me.'

'Jack, there are thousands of books on every subject known to man,' he said. 'So, what can possibly be so important about this one that you are prepared to endanger your life by stealing?'

'Look at this.' I squeezed up next to him and opened it at the page of me introducing Oliver to Fagin. 'Remember how I told you about these people on the Lady Eugenia? Well, somehow the story is here, written down for all to read.'

The look on his face said he thought I was being ridiculous. He took the book from my hands and stared at the picture for a long while before slowly turning the pages. He let out a low whistle.

'You are right, you're name is here, many times. Are you sure you did not know this story before we met? Is this the tale of another that you have taken as your own history?'

'Alfie! You know well that I could not read before I met you.'

'Then who is this man Charles Dickens? Have you spoken to him?'

'Me?' I said, open-mouthed. 'Oh yes, of course, I have. I am always chatting to famous authors at luncheons and garden parties. Alfie, how would the likes of me meet a famous writer?'

He turned back to the first page.

'Will they miss it?'

I nodded. 'In time, for sure.'

'Then how long do we have, for it is a weighty tome with many pages?'

'One week of nights at most,' I said, 'and all day Sunday.'

'Then we had better begin,' says he.

I snuck away before dawn, taking the book with me for fear of it being discovered if I left it in the shed and Alfie got the blame for stealing it.

As he slid the bolt shut, I felt piercing eyes upon me that sent shivers down my back. Peering into darkness, I froze at the reflection of two dark eyes staring out from the bushes.

At first, I thought it was a dingo, and scrabbled about on the ground for a stone to throw at it. Then the clouds scudded away, the moon burst out full and I glimpsed a face.

Not a dingo, but Dungara.

Without the slightest rustling, he was gone like phantom.

With each reading, Oliver's story unfolded in alarming fashion, for what Mr Dickens had written was true in almost every detail, and could only have come from the mouths of Oliver, Mr Brownlow and Fagin himself. As you remember, the pair had visited him in Newgate the night before he was hanged.

It was a story of misery, what with his mother dying as he was born, life in the workhouse under the cruel Mr Bumble the Beadle, working for Sowerberry the undertaker, from whom he had escaped when I took pity on him as he limped along the Watford Road. As Alfie read, there were moments when I almost felt sorry for the orphaned boy, but he weren't alone in having had a hard childhood. It was common for our class, who never knew their parents or any life other than poverty, misery and thieving.

What I hated with a passion were the drawings by Mr George Cruickshank who did no favours to Fagin and gave me the appearance of a monkey. I admit I'm no winner in the beauty stakes, but nor did I resemble the ape-like creature in his sketches.

On the fourth night, Alfie gave me the news that Grimshaw had been to see him.

'Queer,' he said, 'he was in a good mood and quite respectful for a change. He says that when Mr McIntyre returns from Sydney I shall be moved to a new job inside the house.'

'That's good,' I said. 'Better than this hovel.'

Alfie shook his head. 'I worked as an engraver before my crimes,' he said sadly. 'Always inside, never out. Now, I have come to love the garden and feeling the sun on my face and nurturing the plants. They have become my friends and I will miss them sorely. Not this shed, for my old bones and lungs cannot take too much more. Even so, I cannot believe he has anything good in store for me. I tell you straight, I am afraid, Jack.'

'Your mates will still look after you,' I said, though we had no chance of taking him food once he had been moved. In fact, I couldn't see what power we had to do anything for him.

The sky was reddening with the dawn as I was slipping the latch on the barracks door using a bent nail, another dodge learned at Fagin's Academy for Felons, when the hair on the back of my neck prickled up. Someone was near, watching, and for sure it would be Dungara, lurking in the bushes, as he had done on every night I'd visited the shed. Before I could warn him off, a hand clamped itself over my mouth, and when I tried to duck away, an arm wrapped itself around my body, hurling me against the trunk of a tree, knocking the wind from my lungs.

'One peep an' I'll slit yer skinny gizzard. Nod if you understand.'

It was none other than Hobbs.

Preferring not to have my throat cut, I did as he said.

'You're up to something, young Dodger, and I want to know what.'

'Nothing!' I said. 'Leastways nothing you don't know about, since you and all the others have been giving me grub for Alfie.'

He pushed his face into mine. 'You've been five hours away from your bed. The same on the last three nights. No man misses his sleep for nought.'

I said, 'I keep the old boy company. You know we were friends on the Lady Eugenia, and on the road gang. He's like a father to me.' I became bolder. 'In any case, what does it matter to you?'

His hand tightened around my throat. 'Hold your noise. You're planning something. You,

Watchit and the posh 'un, Radley. Me and my mates think you're going to make a break for China. You spoiled our last chance by getting caught. We want to be in on this one.'

'You're wrong,' I said, 'we've never even thought about it, let alone talked. Anyway, I'd rather see out the time I've got left and be set free rather than shot or hanged.'

He had made up his mind and wasn't in the mood for believing anything else. 'In that library where you're working there's maps and all sorts. You can get tools, and the posh 'un can get horses. It has to be, and Watchit is the mastermind. Don't try to tell me otherwise.'

I wanted to be sick. 'Hobbs,' I said, in a voice that was all reasonableness, 'Alfie is not fit for such an adventure, his lungs are shot and he spits blood. He cannot walk a mile let alone get over the Blue Mountains. As for me, do you think I'd be involved with anything like that again when I still carry the weals on my back from the last time?'

The door creaked and Hobbs jumped away as Radley's head came poking through the gap.

'Jack? Is that you? I was getting worried.'

'Jonathan,' I said, relieved, 'I'm glad to see you.'

He saw Hobbs. 'What's going on?'

'We were just chatting,' said Hobbs. 'About nothing in particular.'

Radley pushed between us. 'If there's something on your mind, you'd best tell me, and leave Jack alone.'

Hobbs shook his head. 'Nothing as might concern you, my fine posh friend.' He pushed past and entered the barracks.

'What did he want?' asked Radley.

'He thinks we're planning an escape,' I said, 'and him and his mates want to be in on it.'

Radley never said a word, which I thought were a bit peculiar.

Alfie read to me all week and right through Sunday into the night. When we had finished, I knew Oliver Twist's life story better than he knew it himself. What a tale it was, ending happily for Oliver who was adopted by his grandfather, Mr Brownlow, but not for Nancy, Fagin or Bill Sikes. That pair of criminals got their just desserts, but Nancy, who was a living angel dragged into the gutter by poverty, didn't deserve such a horrible end. It was also curious that in all those hundreds of pages Mr Dickens scarcely mentions my mate Charley Bates until the very last page. It turns out that Charley was so shocked by Sikes murdering Nancy that he decided honesty was the best policy and gave up thieving forthwith. Going straight after a life of crime ain't no easy task, there's temptations everywhere and many fail, but Charley struggled to make honest wages and became a grazier[15] in Northamptonshire. Good luck, I say. It takes courage to do what he did and I do believe that Mr D put him in as an example of what a

---

[15] A farmer who fattens cattle or sheep on grazing land

determined person can achieve. P'raps it's a foolish thought but, somehow, I couldn't help feeling he was leaving a personal message for me.

'Well, Jack,' said Alfie, gently closing the covers and laying the book in his lap, 'what a saga! He must be quite a fellow this Charles Dickens, that he can find out all this and write it down with such truth. Some of it is hard to believe. Is it really true?'

It wasn't surprising that Alfie should ask such a question, what with some of the goings on in that book, and some of the queer characters on its pages. Ordinary men and women not of the criminal classes would never have come across the likes of 'em.

'Where I am in the story, it is certainly true,' I said. 'I can swear to it, so there's reason to suppose that the other parts are false. But why did he write it, that's what I want to know?'

Alfie became very thoughtful.

'Those with money can afford to buy books,' he said. 'Often, they are people of influence who can bring about changes. Even as we sit here in our prison there are good men and women fighting to stop young children working, who want free education for all, prisons reformed and transportation to this place stopped. If you like, they want to rid the world of such evils as beset the poor and needy. Mr William Wilberforce[16] did

---

[16] 1759-1833, a Member of Parliament and social reformer who successfully outlawed slavery in the West Indies in 1807 and pushed

not give up his cause until he had brought about an end to the slave trade. Perhaps Mr Dickens is alerting influential people to a world they do not know in the hope of pricking their consciences into action.'

'P'raps he's a-trying,' I snorted, 'but the upper classes don't give a tinker's cuss for the likes of us. Do you think that by the time McIntyre has read Oliver Twist he will feel kindly towards the likes of us who have been brought here to make even him richer?'

'Jack, you have often told me of your meeting with Mr O'Connell, and how he took pity on you and your fellows and bought you pie and beer.'

'He could afford it! What's a few shillings to him?'

'Do not be unkind! At that moment, he did what he could and well you know it. You have even called him a saint.' Alfie was angry with me, and quite right too. 'I have read in journals about Mr O'Connor, his newspaper and his organisation called the Chartists, which fights for the rights of the lower classes.' Alfie voiced his words more sternly than anything I heard him say before or after. 'When you are poor it is easy to think that no one cares but, mark my words, one day, because of the likes of Mt O'Connell, they will no longer hang men for stealing bread to fill the stomachs of their starving children, or transport

---

for the abolition of slavery in the British Empire which came about in 1833

them so that their families are cast into lives of poverty and crime. These horrors will be stopped by good men.'

'How do you know all this?' I felt bad about what I had said. 'You speak like a man of education, a parliamentarian.'

He laughed. 'I learned to read when I was a lad. To read is to understand the world.' He took up the book. 'Now, you must return this before it is too late.'

To tell the truth, I didn't want to put the book back in McIntyre's library. I felt it belonged to me, that I had a right to it.

I still had *Oliver Twist* tucked into my waistband, hidden by my jacket, when I arrived at the workshop on Monday morning.

'No time to delay,' warned Henry, wagging a finger. 'Put the tools into the bag, and let's be off. Grimshaw was here not a minute ago and he wants the work in the library finished today.'

Walking to the house, the book scorched my skin like a branding iron, and I feared that the words *Oliver Twist by Charles Dickens* would be burned on my flesh forever. Then I thought, what if I don't put it back? How would McIntyre know I'd pinched it? No one, not even Henry, knew. It would just be a missing book, and he had bigger things to worry about. He would ask his secretary to write to the bookseller in England saying they had forgotten to pack it and, being a good customer, they would put a new copy on the next ship from London without asking any questions. In a year, if all went well, *Oliver Twist* would arrive and that would be that.

'Pardon me, Henry,' I said, suddenly dropping the tool bag and clutching my stomach as if in severe pain. 'I'm feeling real queasy. I think I'm going to be sick.' Before he could utter a word of protest, I put my hand over my mouth and legged it at top speed.

I knew exactly where to hide the book. Snatching a strip of canvas on the way out, I snuck round the back to where newly cut timber was stacked to dry under a lean-to shelter. No one went there except Henry and me and the thick sawn planks, spaced with logs to let the air flow round them, would not be moved for at least twelve months. I found a good place, wrapped the canvas round the book and slid it into a gap between two pieces, pushing it away the full length of my arm. It was dark in the hole and, as hard as I tried, it was impossible to see anything.

Satisfied, I looked about and, seeing all was clear, rounded the workshop and dropped into a bush where I could keep cavy to see if anyone approached the shelter. Hardly daring to draw breath, I waited a full ten minutes.

Nothing stirred. I had not been seen.

Henry was relieved to see me back as I made ugly faces and bent over double to prove I was still in terrible pain.

It was late afternoon before McIntyre and Grimshaw arrived, stretched a hand towards me and snapped his fingers.

'The list. Hurry.'

I handed it over, resisting the urge to dodge the two gold rings on his fingers. Old habits die hard. He riffled through the pages, running a pencil down the edge where I had ticked off the books.

'*Oliver Twist?*'

'Not here, Mr McIntyre, sir,'

'You've checked the boxes?'

'Empty, sir. Everything is laid out before you.'

'You've checked twice.'

'Yes, sir.'

'I have also looked in the boxes, sir,' chipped in Henry. 'They are completely empty.'

McIntyre tossed aside the list and sniffed. 'How inconvenient. I met a man in Sydney who had read it. He told me it was marvellous, so exciting it had kept him up reading long into the night. He described to me such fantastical characters you wouldn't believe could exist on this earth.' He was becoming quite excited. 'There's a Jew called Fagin, a criminal who has an army of boys stealing for him. He meets a bad end, as do many others. It is a novel of course, made up out of the author's head, but would you believe that he describes a young pickpocket called the Artful Dodger, who is transported to this very place. Can you imagine! When I heard that I could hardly wait to get back and read it.' He laughed loudly. 'Funny, as soon as he described this Artful Dodger fellow I immediately thought of you, Dawkins. You were convicted of picking pockets, were you not?'

I nodded, 'Yes, sir, indeed that was my crime and I am sorry to have sinned. I read the Bible every day and say prayers for forgiveness at night.' I didn't, of course, but chat like that always goes down well with those self-righteous beasts who have authority over our lives believe the Ten Commandments are rules only for the poor.

'But, then, it's only a story, eh.' He clapped his hands together. 'I shall write to Foyles in London requesting a replacement. You, Mr Grimshaw, may now supervise placing the books on the shelves, making sure to leave the proper space for the missing volume when it arrives.'

Without further ado, the pair were gone and I heaved a blessed sigh of relief.

'Are you alright?' asked Henry. 'You went white as a sheet while he was talking to you.'

'It's my guts,' I said, larding on the agony. 'It must have been the kangaroo stew we had for supper last night. I ain't exactly feeling tip-top.'

Knowing the book was safe and that I could read it anytime I wanted made me feel better. It was as if a bad puzzle had been solved which, in a way, it had. There again, it had also caused problems, and things were niggling away in my head like burrowing worms.

Mostly, I was called Jack or Dawkins but now and then Hobbs and his pals called me Dodger. I was fearful that one day McIntyre or Grimshaw would hear and put two and two together. Even if they didn't, when a new copy arrived and he discovered that Dodger and Jack Dawkins were one and the same, the game would be up. They would believe I had nicked the book to hide my identity and it would be the worse for me.

Alfie was moved to the house the day McIntyre returned from Sydney and we wondered if we would ever set eyes on the old chap again. We had no reason to go into the house without permission and, if caught, would be up before a magistrate on charges of thieving or worse.

We had settled into new a routine where time passed neither fast nor slow but came and went, the days turning into weeks, the weeks into months. Never once did any of us catch sight of Alfie, until the day Henry and me were ordered to build a platform in the attic of the big house, and there he was, large as life and looking fitter than when I'd last seen him, but not happier.

The attic was a workshop with the sun pouring through a skylight on to a table where Alfie was hunched over a metal plate, working with engraving tools and an enlarging glass. I knew what he was doing because Fagin knew a jeweller in Hatton Garden who could alter the names and patterns on stolen silverware so that it couldn't be recognised, even by the real owner.

'Alfie!' I shouted, overjoyed at seeing the old boy.

'Jack!' he replied, looking up surprised, but casting his eyes down immediately.

'Silence!' shouted Grimshaw bringing his riding crop down with a crack on Alfie's table. 'No talking to him,' he said looking from me to Henry. 'And you,' he spoke directly to Alfie, 'I don't want to hear you speaking to them neither. Now, all of you get on with what you're here for.'

He handed Henry a drawing showing the platform and stamped off to a corner where he sat in a chair and watched our every move. From that moment on, we were never left alone with Alfie.

Henry walked around, studying the drawing, jumping up and down, testing the strength of the beams.

In the corner, under the slope of the roof lay a straw mattress and blankets, a table with cup, plate and spoon, and a chair. Next to the chimneybreast stood a washstand with a jug, bowl and towel, and a chamber pot where Alfie did his business. There was a lock on the door and it was plain to see that he was a prisoner twice over.

'I hope the floor will support what it has to carry,' Henry observed, 'for the platform itself will be heavy.'

'Mind your business!' shouted the overseer. 'Be quiet unless you've got something useful to say.'

Once or twice during that first day, I caught Alfie's eye and he winked to let me know he was well and not to worry. However, it didn't take a blind donkey to know his situation weren't right and that he was just trying to keep me happy.

By the middle of the week, Henry had prepared the timbers, cut the joints and we were assembling the platform, when Grimshaw called us to help a group of convicts struggling with three large wooden cases that had lain under canvas outside the house since the delivery by ox cart.

The cons were sent packing without seeing what the boxes contained, and Henry and me were instructed to lever the boards apart.

'Take care not to damage them packing cases, carpenter,' warned Grimshaw, 'and stack them carefully for they shall be required again.'

Inside was iron machinery, black with gold-painted decoration, the toothed wheels oiled and gleaming. I had never seen the likes, and hadn't a clue what it could do.

When we had left the house for the night, I asked Henry if he knew what it was.

He looked puzzled. 'I saw a newspaper being printed once, on apparatus just like that. It's called a press. I suppose it will sit on our platform, which is why we have made it so strong.'

'Why would McIntyre want such a thing?' I asked. 'There is no one here to write a newspaper, and hardly a soul to read it, even supposing they had the money to buy a copy.'

'It can print anything,' he said. 'Books, posters, the pamphlets people hand out in the streets. But, why here of all places? It is a mystery.' He looked at me sternly. 'And one that I do not intend solving. It is none of our business, Jack. We are tools, like the hammer and saw, which can neither see nor hear and must simply do their job.'

My criminal upbringing had made me nosey and suspicious, but I well understood Henry's reasons for not being curious, and I didn't blame him, so I put it aside until a very odd thing happened.

The pieces of the press had to be lifted on to the platform, and bolted together. Convicts always did the donkeywork, so I couldn't believe my eyes when McIntyre and Grimshaw took off their coats, rolled up their sleeves, and sweated along like navvies with just me, Henry and Alfie.

It was a very unusual situation.

As we were heaving and straining, I felt a hand slip inside my trouser pocket and withdraw immediately. Alfie was on my left, and I knew that it could only have been him. One thing was sure, he was too clumsy to have made a living dipping on the streets of London, but no one had seen.

I daren't look at what he'd put there until after supper when I snuck off and found a tightly folded wad of paper, which I opened with shaking hands. It looked like a bank note, all fancy letters and scrolls, though badly made on the cheap paper that had wrapped the printing press. Underneath I recognised Alfie's letters spelling out the words, *Jonathan will know what to do.*

Jonathan understood immediately.

'It resembles a government bond,' he said. 'See, here is the crown and this fine building is the Bank of England in Threadneedle Street. Its value is one hundred pounds.'

'What is a bond?' I asked, not having a clue about government matters 'ceptin' that it's always best to steer clear if you can.

'Bonds are like money,' he explained. 'When governments need money for the army, or to construct a great building like those in Whitehall, they borrow it from rich people who receive a note like this, promising repayment with interest.'

'Fagin used to lend money to villains,' I said. 'He'd make 'em put their cross on an IOU.'

'It's more or less the same thing, only I suspect that the government is more reliable when it comes to paying the money back.'

'Alfie was transported for forging government bonds,' I said. 'He told me his crime was so severe it was a wonder he weren't hanged for it.'

Radley's face was grim as he waved the sheet in front of me. 'As I remember it, Alfie's bonds were near perfect. I think this means that McIntyre is forcing him to forge bonds,' he said. 'He has already engraved the metal plate from which they can be printed. Tens, perhaps hundreds of thousands of pounds worth.'

It don't look right,' I said pointing to the paper. 'I ain't the Governor of the Bank of England, but even I can tell it don't look like the genuine article. Nobody, even a blind geezer, would accept it.'

'Alfie made this by laying a sheet of rough paper over the engraved plate and scribbling on it with a pencil until the image showed through. If his reputation is anything to go by, when printed on a press using the right ink and paper it will be impossible to tell from the real thing.'

Even if I didn't understand, I was intelligent enough to know that trouble was brewing.

'It is very clever,' said Radley, voice tailing off as he screwed the paper into a ball. 'We must destroy this, for there is great danger afoot.'

'Danger?'

'Who knows about the press?'

'McIntyre and Grimshaw, Alfie, Henry and me.'

'McIntyre and Grimshaw do not know about me, but you three have seen too much. Once Alfie finishes the plates and prints the bonds, he will be of no further use to them. In fact…'

'What are you trying say?' I said, fearing that I already knew his next words.

'I do not think they will want a witness to their crime. Someone who might talk and could send them to prison for life, or the gallows.'

It seems that even amongst criminals there is one law for the rich and another for the poor.

'They can't be transported,' I said. 'I mean, where will they send 'em, England?'

'This is no time for joking,' he said, 'we must think.'

'However, now that you come to mention it,' I said, getting into a funk, 'being witnesses also applies to Henry and me. We have seen Alfie at work and seen the press. That pair ain't going to trust us to keep our mouths shut.'

'I told you, Jack, there is grave danger.'

I took the ball of paper and tossed it from one hand to another, thinking. 'He has written that you will know what to do. So, what's to be done?'

He sighed and shook his head. 'I must come up with a plan.'

'Then be quick,' I told him, 'for you are making me nervous with all your talk of witnesses and danger.'

Chapter 14: Crime and Punishment

In my experience, life seldom goes as planned and, when things do take a turn, it's usually for the worse. That's how it was with *Oliver Twist*.

Someone had been stealing liquor from the store in the big house. When McIntyre found out he flew into a screaming rage and had Grimshaw ranting around the estate threatening a hundred lashes for every man unless it was found and the thief given up for trial and punishment.

The long and short of it was that when no one peached, McIntyre brought in a gang of settlers from the small farms around and about and ordered a search, believing that if the culprits were allowed to get away with their crime Good Hope would become lawless.

Sparing none of our few belongings, they turned over the barracks, upending beds, slitting mattresses and blankets, searching the roof and every nook and cranny. Most of the lags had stuff that weren't allowed. I had the half sovereign I'd lifted from the sergeant on the road, but it was well hidden and they found nothing. They ransacked the garden sheds and greenhouses, scattering flowerpots and canes, searching under bushes for newly turned earth, even sticking the compost heap with pitchforks. Henry's workshop was next and we were made to stand outside while they emptied cupboards, cleared shelves, and tipped over barrels of nails and wood shavings on to the floor. I felt truly sorry for Henry who was a stickler for keeping everything spick and span.

My heart sank when McIntyre ordered his men to search the timber stacks and to pass canes through any gap wide enough to hold a liquor jar.

I held my breath. They might have been seeking stolen liquor, but McIntyre was going to get a surprise when the missing copy of *Oliver Twist* turned up. Considering where it was, they wouldn't have to look far to find the culprit. I just hoped they'd believe me when I said that Henry wasn't involved. We had no choice but to stand and watch. Then, the cry I had been dreading.

'Look! Mr McIntyre, sir, look here!'

I closed my eyes in terror.

'What is it?'

'There's a blockage.'

I squinted through one eye, to see a man poking deep into the timbers with a cane, which weren't going as far as he expected.

'I believe someone has stashed his ill-gotten gains inside the pile.'

'Pull it out!' called McIntyre.

Grimshaw stepped up. 'The gap is too narrow for bottles or jugs, sir. It looks more like a cloth of some kind. If only I could get my fingers round it.'

McIntyre would show no mercy and I could feel the soldiers tricing me to a frame, and hear the swish of the cat as her tails slit my back open.

I dared not look, heard Grimshaw puffing and panting, then shout. 'Got it!'

'Well, well, well,' I heard McIntyre say. 'It seems that we do not have one thief on the estate, but two. What's in the bag, Mr Grimshaw?'

Bag? A length of raggy canvas wasn't a bag.

I dared a peep.

Grimshaw was pulling an assortment of weapons from a canvas bag, tossing them to the ground at his feet.

'It seems we have a would-be escaper amongst us, Mr McIntyre,' he said with a smile as the pile grew.

McIntyre was blazing mad. 'Find whoever put this here, and let's have him in front of a magistrate without delay. We're going to skin every inch of flesh from his back. Now, let's get on to the bakery and find that liquor.'

I could not believe my luck when they stormed off, satisfied with having found the guns and not bothering to look further.

It weren't many days before two mysteries were solved at one and the same time.

McIntyre was acting like a mad man. All he cared about was who had stolen his liquor and for days the whole estate had stopped work to search until there was hardly a place left to look.

We were fixing the five bar gate that closed off the road to the great house, when there was a regular uproar, bawling and screaming the likes of which I hadn't heard outside of the scrapping that went on outside rough Whitechapel taverns. It was coming from the direction of the aborigine village, which the searchers had left until last.

McIntyre and Grimshaw were leading a tail of noisy aborigines towards the house, and it didn't take a bright spark to see that the pair of them were very angry.

McIntyre was dragging the old chief by the hair with one hand, and carrying two clinking bottles of rum in the other. The old boy looked well boozed and weren't putting up much of a struggle. Grimshaw followed, tugging Dungara by a rope round his neck. The boy's hands were tied, and when he stumbled and fell to his knees, Grimshaw gave him two sharp kicks in the ribs, hauled him to his feet, punched his face and yanked the rope tight, almost choking him.

All through it, Dungara's face never changed. He just stared at Grimshaw with hatred burning deep in his eyes.

I caught my breath. Under Grimshaw's arm I could see a book with a red cover. Even at that distance, I knew what it was. *Oliver Twist*.

No wonder they hadn't found it in the woodpile. It hadn't been there.

I knew Dungara might have followed me to the shelter to watch what I was doing and, too clever to be tricked by a foreign town boy, he must have waited until I'd gone to see what I'd hidden.

I smacked my head, furious at my own stupidity. But when had he taken it? After I had hidden it or later? Whatever he had done, for the moment his foolishness had got me off the hook.

When he stumbled again, Grimshaw set about him with his riding crop, thrashing the boy's bare skin and drawing blood, and kicking him for good measure. The aborigines surrounded them, pushing and shoving though not daring to pull Grimshaw off for fear of being lashed themselves.

The pair were hauled to a stone shed with an iron door where prisoners were locked up until the magistrate arrived. It reminded me of the cell in the yard of the court where I had sobbed my heart out while waiting to be taken to Newgate.

The pair of 'em meant nothing to me, nevertheless I felt for 'em because I'd tasted what they had coming.

Twenty yards away, a dab of red in the dust caught my eye. *Oliver Twist* was lying where it had fallen during the scuffle.

Henry was staring after the crowd.

'Who'd have thought them aborigines would have done the stealing,' he said. 'I should've guessed at Hobbs and company myself.'

I didn't answer, but strolled all nonchalant into the road, stooped as if tying a bootlace, and stuffed the book inside my jacket.'

'What have you got there?' said Henry as I returned to the gate.

I thought he hadn't noticed. 'Nothing.'

'I saw you pick something up and put it inside your coat. Come on, Jack, what's going on. You'd best tell me.'

Henry had me banged to rights and the lump under my jacket proved it. I had no option but to show him the book tucked into my waistband.

He whistled. 'Would that be the missing *Oliver Twist* by any chance?'

'Looks like,' I said.

Henry shook his head. 'Well I'll be blowed. I can understand 'em nicking liquor, but a book? None of 'em can speak English let alone read it, so what could Dungara have been thinking of? You'd better catch 'em up and give it to Mr McIntyre.'

I shook my head. 'No!'

He was taken aback at my sharp answer.

'What do you mean, no?'

'I mean he's not having it, it's mine!'

'The book is not yours as well you know. You must return it before he discovers it missing a second time, as he surely will.'

'I will not.'

Henry might have been from the West Country and a bit slow catching on, but even he could smell that something wasn't quite in order.

'You're not being straight with me,' he said. 'Why ain't you telling me the truth?'

'I'm keeping it,' I said. 'That's all there is about it, and I'll call upon your friendship not to peach.'

There was sadness in Henry's eyes when I said that, and he bit his lower lip to stop himself speaking. For the likes of me to suggest that he might turn me in to Grimshaw was unforgivable, and I wouldn't have blamed him if he'd balled his fist and knocked out my teeth. I was in the wrong. Henry was a decent sort who didn't deserve such lip from an oik like me.

Things were warming up at Good Hope and before we knew it, someone had peached on Hobbs, fingering him for stashing the weapons found in the timber pile.

They locked him up in the cell next to Dungara.

The next thing, a carriage containing two men in black suits and stovepipe hats, accompanied by a troop of soldiers in an open cart, rolled up to the house. Stealing on the streets of London gives you a nose for Peelers and their ilk, and these were the law without the shadow of a doubt. Word soon went round that they were a magistrate and his clerk come to try Dungara, the Chief and Hobbs.

The following morning a table and two chairs were set up in front of the house, upon which the clerk laid out official books and papers.

Chairs were set a few yards behind the table for McIntyre and Grimshaw, and we cons were arranged in rows behind them, perfectly positioned to see the whipping frame erected by the soldiers to punish those found guilty. Soldiers, with muskets poised, faced us just to make sure we didn't get up to any tricks.

'All stand!' bellowed the clerk. Only McIntyre and Grimshaw rose, the rest of us not having been provided with the luxury of chairs.

The magistrate, whose name was Samuel Hardcastle, emerged from the house, sat down and adjusted his spectacles across a nose resembling a ripe, purple plum.

'Bring out the first accused,' he ordered.

Two soldiers marched Hobbs, hands and feet shackled, in front of the magistrate.

'Say your name?' said Hardcastle.

'You know it well enough,' said Hobbs, spitting into the dust.

Hardcastle was not impressed. A thousand felons had appeared before him, he'd seen their antics and, no matter what the prisoner said, he would have the last word, usually, with a whip.

'William Hobbs,' said the clerk, 'serving twenty years for cattle stealing, and charged with possessing weapons in an attempt to escape.'

'How do you plead?' asked Hardcastle.

'And what difference do it make what I say?' snarled Hobbs. 'You've already judged me guilty.'

'Witnesses?' asked Hardcastle, looking around.

'The one who found the weapons, sir,' said the clerk. 'Shall I call him?'

The witness was called, and duly swore on the Bible that he had found the bag of weapons shown to him by the clerk.

'Will you testify that these were the illegal property of the defendant?' asked Hardcastle.

The witness was a settler from a nearby farm who wouldn't have known Hobbs from Mr Martin van Buren, President of Yankeeland.

'I cannot, sir,' he replied honestly. 'I only found the bag and do not know its owner. Nor have I ever seen that man before.'

'No matter,' said Hardwick, dismissing him with a flick of the hand. 'William Hobbs, I find you guilty of these serious charges and sentence you to one hundred and fifty lashes to be administered immediately after this court, and twenty years to be added to your sentence. Take him away.'

I thought I'd seen rough justice in London, but if I'm to believe that Hobbs had been given what they called a fair trial, then Fagin would have been a saint sitting alongside St Peter in Heaven.

Worst of it was, as they marched him off, he looked at me and hissed, 'I'll have you for peaching, and when you wake one morning with your throat cut, you'll know who done it and why.'

That was my reputation done up like a kipper for there wasn't a con there who hadn't heard his every word and believed it. In their eyes, I had committed the greatest sin of all, peaching.

Next, they dragged out the chief and went through the same rigmarole of asking his name and charging him with theft. That he couldn't speak a word of English, nor understand what was being said, never seemed to bother anyone.

'Say your name,' said Hardcastlc.

The chief never moved.

'We have no name,' said the clerk.

'Witnesses?' asked Hardcastle.

'The land owner, Mr McIntyre, will give evidence against the accused,' announced the clerk, at which McIntyre jumped to his feet. 'Take the Bible in your right hand and swear after me.' McIntyre repeated that he promised to tell the truth, the whole truth and nothing but the truth.

'What do you know, Mr McIntyre?'

'A great deal of liquor has been disappearing from the cellar of the house. After searching the aborigine village, the accused was found drunk, with two bottles of estate rum in his possession and a great many empties behind his shack.'

'Who found him?'

'I did.'

Without further ado the old chap was sentenced to one hundred lashes, and on Hardwick's instructions, his badge of rank was removed.

Dungara never took his eyes off me as he was marched to the table. He knew he hadn't nicked the book, it already being stolen property when he laid hands on it. The question was, who should have been standing there, me or him?

When asked his name, he didn't answer. Like the Chief, he neither understood nor spoke

English, though I suspect he had a good idea why he was there and, if he chose, he could point out the real culprit. I trembled at the thought.

Both McIntyre and Grimshaw gave evidence against him. As they were telling how he was always lurking outside the library and that they'd found the book in his hut, he looked sideways over his shoulder, watching me from the corner of his eye. You can bet your boots, I was glad that he couldn't speak our lingo and couldn't involve me.

Hardcastle was not interested in anything Dungara might have wanted to say, only in finding him guilty as quickly as possible, but even he smelled a rat because, before passing sentence, he peered over the top of his spectacles at the boy and spoke slowly and loudly, 'Can you speak English, boy?'

Dungara didn't move a muscle.

'If you cannot speak English, then why did you steal a book?'

Dungara didn't even blink.

'They're an ignorant lot, these aborigines!' shouted Grimshaw, a grin splitting his ugly chops. 'P'raps he thought he could eat it!'

They had a good laugh, even the cons who didn't give a toss about his fate. Hardwick looked at his watch, decided it had all taken too long, and sentenced him to one hundred strokes.

They were lashed in the order of trial. Hobbs first, cursing me for a peaching devil as they stripped off his shirt and triced him to the frame. He only shut his bawling when the first stroke of the cat tore his back. I had imagined him for a coward but never once during that dreadful beating did he cry out, nor lose his senses and, when they cut him free, he shrugged off the guards and walked away by himself on shaking legs. When he fell into the dust, he brushed away the soldiers' hands, picked himself up and continued unaided. He was a tough one, no messing.

The Chief passed out on the third lash but it never stopped them giving him the full hundred. I thought he was dead when they cut him down and the villagers carried him off.

Dungara, too, was made of stern stuff.

As the soldiers triced him up, stretching his arms until the skin was taut across his back, my head was bursting with thoughts that I should shout a confession and call a halt to matters. My eyes were screwed shut when I heard the whistle of the whip and the leather tails ripping his back.

He never uttered a sound throughout them dreadful proceedings and, as they dragged him off, torn and bleeding, he kept his eyes firmly on mine.

What had I done?

What had I done!

It ought to have been me hanging there, not a foolish aborigine who had pinched nothing from McIntyre and was being punished for it.

Chapter 15: Outcast

To say I became an outcast wouldn't be telling the half of it. The cons, with the exception of Radley, stopped talking to me and hissed *scum, rat, peacher* and worse whenever they came within earshot, believing I had shopped Hobbs to get my own back for the lashing on the Lady Eugenia. After a while I gave up protesting my innocence and kept to myself as much as was possible in that place.

Henry spoke but only when necessary, to ask me to fetch this or carry that, but we never had chats like before and he gave up teaching me the tools. I didn't blame him a gnat's whisker because apart from Dungara, he was the one person who knew for sure that I had more to do with the disappearance of *Oliver Twist* than I was letting on.

'It ain't right,' he told me burning with anger. 'You could've stopped it but chose not to.'

At that, I got all uppity and said, 'Well, I ain't taking lectures from no murderer, that's for sure.'

I regretted opening my big trap immediately.

'I am not a murderer,' he replied quietly. 'And you have no right to suggest it.'

'You said you were sent here for doing murder.'

'I told you I was *sentenced* for murder,' he said, a tear in the corner of his eye. 'The court found me guilty right enough, for a crime I did not commit.'

'Pull the other one,' I sneered. 'They all say that. The barracks is full of innocent men.'

'You are free to believe whatever you choose,' he said, picking up a chisel and feeling the edge with his thumb. 'But whatever I did or didn't do, don't make what you've done right. That's for your conscience. Think about it, Jack Dawkins.'

It's terrible thing being forced to listen to the truth. It was miserable.

At night, I lay on my bunk in the dark while Hobbs' mates taunted me with threats of what would befall me if I dared to fall asleep. Radley tried to warn them off, but they took no notice.

To tell the truth I was scared to death of what was going to happen.

After a couple of weeks, Hobbs was up and about, walking at the crouch as the scabs on his back stiffened. Often there were smears of blood on his shirt where the wounds broke open as he moved. Not that I could bring myself to feel sorry for him. He had not given me a thought on the ship, and I weren't the one who'd peached on him.

Dungara was also healing and most days sat outside the workshop where he never took his eyes off me. The queer thing was, they were not filled with hatred as mine would have been were our positions reversed. I could've stood that, or him calling me vile names like the others, but just sitting there without saying a word grated on my nerves. All I could imagine was that he was biding his time before taking revenge.

With all the goings-on, *Oliver Twist* seemed to have been forgotten, and even when Henry and me were called up to the house to repair the platform, neither McIntyre nor Grimshaw mentioned it, probably because they were too busy with other dirty business.

It was plain to see that the press had been working, because there was paper everywhere, much of it screwed up in balls and tossed on a large pile in the corner. It took me, McIntyre, Grimshaw and Alfie to support a corner while Henry fitted a new leg.

When I felt a hand in my pocket, I knew that Alfie had slipped me another note. I was not happy because I had enough problems as it was.

Only five people knew the secret of what was going on in the attic, and I couldn't help remembering what Radley had said without a shiver running down my spine.

After supper, he took me aside.

'Jack,' he said and, from his tone, I knew something big was afoot. 'Hobbs and his crew and the Irish who worked with them on the bridge are going to escape and have asked me to join them. There will be ten of us in all. You are not included.'

'Will you go?' I asked, shaken by his words. 'You are not good friends with these men and you know they are not trustworthy.'

'I have had enough of this place,' he said. 'Whatever the consequences, I will not spend any more time here. I am prepared to take my chances.'

'At least with Hobbs gone, I shan't be going in fear of my life,' I quipped, trying to make out I never cared a fig.

He put a hand on my shoulder. 'There is no easy way to say this, but on the night we depart Hobbs has vowed to kill you for peaching.'

'I never did such a thing.' I was trembling, I don't mind telling you, and tried to laugh it off by saying, 'Then I'd better go missing myself. My life here is a misery. I was thinking about it anyway.'

'What do you mean?'

I gave him the paper Alfie had slipped into my pocket.

As he opened it his mouth widened in astonishment.

'One thousand pounds!' he let out a low whistle. 'It is a government bond for one thousand pounds!'

'A man would be a king with that much money,' I said. 'And I expect he has printed thousands.'

'You can be certain of it,' said Radley, tracing a finger along the message written in the margin. 'This is bad. Does Henry know?'

I shook my head. 'I have not told him. We are not on speaking terms.'

'You must, and without delay. If what is written here is true, then his life is in danger.' He read every word carefully. 'I was right. Alfie has been forced to forge bonds and knows they will murder him because he knows too much. He warns that you and Henry will receive the same treatment.'

'Then I shall be killed twice over,' I said. 'What it is to be popular, eh, Jonathan!'

In a hundred years, I wouldn't have imagined missing the villainy of Fagin, Sikes and those other Whitechapel cutthroats who were like newborn lambs compared with those at Good Hope.

Radley changed the subject. 'Hobbs and his mates will run at the dark of the moon. The Irish too. They want me to steal horses and believe they can find a way across the Blue Mountains to China.'

'Is it possible?'

'Who knows? But I shall not be relying on them to ensure my freedom.'

'Go with them. Take Alfie and Henry. Make it a condition of helping them. They need you and will not speak against it. I will take my chances.'

Radley was stern. 'I have a better idea, or the beginnings of one. Meantime, pray that McIntyre does not carry out his plans for the government bonds before we have a chance to foil him.'

There weren't much point in me trying to speak to Henry, since he was hardly likely to believe a word I said, so Radley explained everything. To begin with, he didn't want to believe it, and who could blame him because he had never put a toe out of line and did his work as best he could. Radley's speech must have come as quite a shock, and Henry didn't know what to do until he was shown the one thousand pound bond. Then it sunk in and he was as terrified as me.

'I am all for escaping,' said Henry, 'but Alfie should be our greatest concern since we cannot leave him at the mercy of those villains.'

'Then we must find a way of getting him out,' said Radley.

As far as I could see, he might as well have been locked up in the Tower of London. Someone young and quick, like me, could have squeezed out of the skylight, crossed the roof and shinned down a rain pipe, but Alfie was old and would certainly break his neck.

Yet there had to be a way.

There was always a way.

No matter how many locks, bars and guard dogs there were on a house, Sikes and his mates always found a way in. Once, they had pushed Oliver through a small fanlight so that he could open the door from inside. He did manage to wake up the whole house and get himself shot by the owner, but it makes my point. There is always a way.

Alfie had to be told what was afoot and given the same chance as everyone else.

McIntyre's house wasn't guarded. By ten o'clock, the candles were usually doused and the family was in bed. Grimshaw lived in a cottage by himself and, after he'd done his final rounds, turned in for the night.

I was the very man for the job. The idea scared the britches off me yet, at the same time, I was excited by the prospect. Radley nearly fell flat on his face when I suggested breaking into the house and telling Alfie.

'I can pick locks,' I said. 'Another of my many talents. I can shin up drainpipes and squeeze through small places. I can do it, Jonathan and, remember, I have worked in that house many times. I know the layout, where he is and how to get there.'

'It is dangerous. Get caught it won't be a lashing. You'll find yourself dangling at the end of a rope.'

You can imagine what I thought about that, having seen Fagin's bulging eyes and lolling tongue as he swung before the crowd.

'When Henry and me were doing the job in the library, I noticed that the keys are kept in a cupboard near the front door. The attic key will surely be there with all the others. Hobbs's mate, Springer can make keys, he did it on the Lady Eugenia, and he can do it here. You must ask him to get the materials to make impressions.'

'Even so, once Springer had made them we would have to get them to Alfie.'

'Don't worry,' I said, 'I have thought of that. When I enter the house I will tell Alfie where and when, and how he will receive the keys.'

'You seem to have thought of everything,' he said, 'except your own escape.'

I laughed. 'On the night, I shall leave before you and before Hobbs comes to murder me. He will not try anything until the very last moment for fear of it going wrong.'

'And then...?'

'What else but make my way to the sea and board a Yankee whaler. Perhaps Mr Martin van Buren is looking for talented chaps like me who can read books.' Straight away, I could see that Radley was against it, but before he could say anything, I held up my hands. 'I ain't taking no for an answer, Jonathan, nothing else makes sense.'

'Do you know the way to the coast?'

I had to admit, he had me there.

'I haven't a clue,' I said, 'But any man who can find his way from Watford to Shoreditch through that maze of streets ain't going to have much trouble finding something as big as the ocean.'

I felt quite girly when he reached out and hugged me. In fact, I was quite tearful.

'You're a good chap, Jack,' he said, 'and we're going to get out of this together, all four of us.'

'But I ain't going with you, Henry and Alfie,' I said. 'Hobbs'll be with you and he'll do for me.'

'Have faith,' he said. 'Do you really think I would let you venture into the wilds on your own, when you haven't the slightest idea where you are heading?'

'Well, I ain't no great shakes with north and south,' I said, offended that he thought I couldn't find my way but relieved by his words.

'We need each other,' he said, 'and shall do this together.'

'I am pleased to hear it,' I said, for the first time in ages feeling happier.

'Good! Then one thing at a time. You told me there are maps in the library. Get a good one, for when we run, it must be in the right direction.'

'Very well, while I am in the house I shall just pop into the library and get what is required,' I said, trying to sound bright and breezy. Oliver had taken a bullet doing a burglary and had nearly croaked. And all he was doing was slipping the latch on the front door to let Sikes in.

The dark of the moon was ten days off when I told Radley that I planned to do the job that very night.

'I know you're thinking,' I said, 'What happens if I'm caught? Well, you can be sure I will keep my mouth shut and take any punishment coming my way. I have proved it in the past.'

'They won't just lash you. They'll add years to your sentence, like Hobbs. Maybe even hang you.' He put his hand on my shoulder. 'Take great care, Jack, and if you are in any doubt, call it off.'

After supper he handed me a battered tin.

'Soap,' he said. 'For the keys. You were right, Hobbs had no choice but to accept Alfie and Henry if they wanted horses. They were suspicious about who would make the impressions and I told them I would be doing it. They are not expecting anything to happen tonight and will not bother you. In any case, I shall leave the barracks as if going to do the job, and hide until you return.'

Not wanting Hobbs and company to become suspicious, I pulled the dodge I'd used on Henry, by lying on my bunk groaning and twisting, which made them angry at the thought of having to listen to me all night, and there were soon calls for me to pack it in or else they'd shut me up for good.

I quietened down and gave it a few minutes until after Grimshaw had done his rounds, counted us twice and locked the door. Not that it made any difference, the lock was simple and an infant could have opened it with a pin.

'I ain't well, my guts are playing me up. I'm going out,' I announced.

They were glad to see the back of me, and Hobbs shouted, 'Good riddance to bad rubbish, I say. And don't puke on the path.'

Creeping from my bunk, I used the bent nail on the lock, closed the door behind me and fled into the bushes, certain that Dungara's beady eyes were following me from the darkness.

A light was showing in Grimshaw's cottage and I lurked in the shadows watching him drink a glass of brandy then lower the flame in the lamp.

Crouching, I ran through the vegetable garden where Alfie had once worked, squeezed into a gap behind the greenhouse, clambered over a wall and dropped down into the yard where merchants slid sacks of flour, beans and salt down a chute into the cellar beneath the kitchen. Henry had warned Grimshaw that the planks in the trapdoor had shrunk with the weather and needed replacing. Thankfully, the overseer had told him that there were more important tasks and to forget it.

I hadn't bargained with the noise as I forced a chisel blade between the door and frame and wiggled it about to find the bolt. Metal squeaked against metal like a rat caught in a trap.

Nervous, I waited to see if anything stirred, keeping one eye on the wall in case Dungara had followed me.

At the fifth try, the bolt moved and I pushed until it snapped open with a clang that had me jumping out of my boots.

Hanging on with one hand, the other holding the trapdoor open, I slithered on to the brass chute. The metal was shiny, the door heavy, my fingers ached and I couldn't get a proper grip. I had no choice but to let go, dropping it with an almighty clang, whacking my head. I cried out, lost my hold and plummeted down to a hard landing on the brick floor, knocking over a pile of boxes, scattering fruit across the cellar.

The racket seemed to go on forever.

In the pitch black, I held my breath.

I heard a window thrown open.

'Who's there?' It was McIntyre, unhappy to have been woken.

A dingo barked.

'Blast those wild dogs!' he shouted. 'Looking for food, that's what it is. They're getting to be a nuisance. Grimshaw'll have to do something about them before we're overrun with the beasts.'

He slammed the window shut.

Shaking as if I'd just bathed in ice, I whipped off my boots and stood them at the end of the chute where I could find them in the dark, and felt my way towards the steep stairs.

One floor up, moonlight was streaming through the kitchen widows.

I breathed deeply, listening to my heart pounding and collecting my thoughts.

First things first. Find the keys, which would be hanging in the cupboard in the boot room between the kitchen and the passage leading to the hall.

I tiptoed along the corridor shaking like a leaf. How Sikes could go burgling every night of the week was beyond me.

A labelled key hung on every peg. In the dark it wasn't easy finding the right ones and I had to carry them a few at a time to the window where there was more light.

I found the pair I wanted, made two impressions, cleaned off all traces of soap and replaced the key to the main door, keeping the one to the attic.

Next, the library. Out of the boot room, along the passage into the hall where the stairs led upwards. It was the last door.

Dozens of rolled maps stood upright in a tub next to the desk where McIntyre wrote his letters. One by one, I pulled them out, carried them to the window, and read the titles by the dim light. In the bottom right hand corner of the seventh, it said *Sydney &New South Wales* in fancy script. I folded it tightly and stuffed it inside my shirt.

The drawers of the desk were locked but it didn't take many moments with a silver paperknife to get 'em open and root about for the compass I had seen while unpacking the boxes.

My word did those stairs creak, a sound that reminded me of the rope squealing against the timbers of the scaffold as Fagin turned in the breeze. No matter how lightly I trod, it was dreadful and I thought that the whole household would hear but, judging by the snoring coming from the rooms as I crept along the landing, it would have taken a broadside from one of Her Majesty's warships to wake them.

The key turned smoothly in the lock to the attic. In a second, I was inside.

The old chap was snoring lightly on the bed in the corner. Gently, I shook him.

He was startled. 'What the…'

I clamped my hand across his mouth.

'Alfie, it is me, Jack. Don't make a sound.'

'I can't see you, it is dark, light the lamp.'

'Best not,' I said, 'for this is no social visit and I will not be stopping for tea and sandwiches, only to give you instructions for your escape.'

He sat upright. 'I am not fully awake. I thought you said *escape*.'

'I showed the bond to Jonathan. We will escape at the dark of the moon, and you will come with us.'

'I meant only to warn you and Henry of the danger. I can guess what those devils have in store for me but I am far too old to run.'

'Well,' I said firmly, 'you can bet your boots we ain't a-taking off without you, and that's a fact.'

'I will slow you down.'

I took no notice, and reached into my pocket for the ball of string taken from the carpentry shop. Pressing it into his hand, I said. 'I do not have much time. Hide this. On the night of the escape, at this very same time, throw one end from the skylight. I will attach a bag containing the keys to this door and the front door. You will haul them up, and let yourself out. Tell me you understand?'

'I understand,' came the firm reply.

'It will happen at the dark of the moon, ten nights from tonight. Repeat it.'

Alfie did.

'Go to the stables where Jonathan will wait for you.'

'I understand.'

'Good. Now I must go. By bye, Alfie.'

'Goodnight, Jack, and thanks to you all.'

I was gone in a flash and downstairs hanging up the key in less than a minute.

When my leather boots wouldn't grip the chute, I tied the laces together, hung them around my neck and went up barefoot.

It was impossible to push the bolt on the trapdoor back into place, so I didn't bother, just lowered it quietly into place then hopped over the back wall and dropped down behind the greenhouse. As my feet hit the ground, I saw something dart round the corner.

Dungara!

I went after the blighter. His name might have meant lightning and he might have been a good runner, but he'd never been chased up Fenchurch Street by a bunch of angry peelers wielding truncheons. I caught up and dived at his feet, bringing him down with me on top, then whacked him a couple of times to stop him wriggling.

'What's your game?' I demanded pinning him by the shoulders. 'Can't I go anywhere without you a-spying on me?'

If he understood, he never showed it nor made a squeak.

'I suppose you'll be telling Grimshaw what I've been up to,' I said, getting up.

He got to his feet and we stood there staring at each other, him with a weird look on his face that could have been anything from a bad smell under his nose to real hatred.

Without warning, he darted left and right, fooling me good and proper, and was gone.

Chapter 16: Escape

It is curious how you can wish for something at the same time as hoping it never comes.

Like the dark of the moon.

As I watched its light getting dimmer by the night, I was excited by the thought of running yet, scared of what might happen. I wished for the days to pass quickly and, also, that they wouldn't.

When the night came, Radley had not fully unfolded his plan, but I trusted him and knew he would do right by me.

All day, the cons were jittery and Grimshaw, who had a nose for sniffing out trouble, knew something was afoot, though he couldn't put his finger on it.

Radley took me aside as the sun was setting and pressed a small sack into my hand.

'These are Alfie's keys. You must go to him immediately after Grimshaw locks us up for the night. Deliver them as you arranged, then make all speed across the new bridge. After a mile, you will come upon a signpost, pointing left to Bathurst, right to Lithgow. Go right, even if you cannot read the sign. In another mile, you will find a copse. Hide there. When you see us arrive, on no account show yourself until I call your name. Repeat what I have said.'

I repeated it without error.

'Good,' he said. 'When you leave the barracks, I'm sure Hobbs will follow. I will delay him as best I can, but you must not dally. Get your business done with Alfie, then do not stop running until you have reached the copse. Good luck, Jack!'

'And you,' I said.

He shook my hand and turned away.

My dodge of pretending to have guts ache was wearing thin, but there was no choice but to use it again. Radley was right. As I left the barracks, I could feel Hobbs watching me.

Outside, I felt more eyes, staring from the dark. I didn't know whether to find out who it was and risk Hobbs appearing, or see if it was Dungara and warn him off. Not wanting the aborigine trailing me and knowing where I'd gone, I nipped behind the building to wait and, sure enough, it weren't long before a figure emerged from behind a tree and started in my direction.

To my horror, it weren't either of 'em but Grimshaw. That devilish overseer didn't miss a trick and his bloodhound nose had served him well. He had witnessed me leaving the barracks and there was no way I could let Radley know he was on the loose.

Time was passing and there was nothing else for it. I felt around for something to whack him with, and came upon the log we used for propping the door open in hot weather. As he snuck round the corner, I let swing with a vengeance and missed. He stumbled, fell and walloped his head on the corner, knocking himself spark out. I had his belt off in double quick time, strapped his wrists behind him, then tied his bootlaces together for good luck. He was heavy but I managed to drag him round the corner to the barracks steps where I rapped on the door, before taking off as fast as my legs could carry me, wishing I could've seen the lags' faces when they found him on their doorstep. Those boys would make sure he stayed trussed up until long after they had departed.

The string was hanging down the wall.

I tied the bag on, gave a couple of jerks, waited for a tug from above and was off as fast as my short legs would carry me, to the back of Alfie's old garden shed, where I'd hidden *Oliver Twist* under flowerpots. With it tucked in my waistband, I made for the new bridge.

The dark of the moon might be the right time to escape because no one can see you, but you can't see much either and there's traps at every step. Bushes, stones, animal holes and fallen branches, any one of 'em can send you head over heels, and it wasn't long before I was tumbling around faster than a circus acrobat. Once or twice, I was seeing more stars than there were in the sky.

I made what speed I could to the fork. The sign was impossible to read, but I turned right checking several times before pushing on. It weren't like running in London where I could outpace the fastest Peeler on pavements, but bumpy and uphill so that my lungs were on fire by the time I came to the copse. It was little more than a dozen trees and some scrubby bushes. I could do nought but hope that I had found the meeting place and Radley and the boys would turn up as promised.

I admit I was frightened as I settled down to wait, listening to the rustling bushes and slithering of animals that had me fearing for being bitten and dying a slowly without a friend to hold my hand. I wondered what would happen if Radley and the rest didn't show up. I would be up a gum tree, not being able to go back for fear of my life, and not knowing if China was right and the ocean left or the other way around. I had no food, no water and, no clue of how to live off the land. I had nothing to make a fire and would probably end up eating grass like the animals, unless one ate me first, which were more than likely.

On the road gang, I'd seen the soldiers firing shots after escapers and they would surely hunt me down in the same fashion.

I was scaring myself silly.

Even so, I must have dozed off, for when I finally heard horses' hooves they were right on top of me.

I wanted to jump out straight away until I heard Hobbs's voice, remembered Radley's words and stayed where I was.

'What's up? Why are you stopping?' Hobbs shouted as the hoof beats slowed. 'We have to keep going and put as many miles between them and us as we can before dawn.'

'Take our horses and go on,' I heard Radley calling back. 'You will be faster without us.'

'I don't trust you, posh boy,' Hobbs growled viciously. 'You've got something up your sleeve.'

'Never mind all that,' came the voice of one of the Irish escapers, 'we don't need him.'

Through the gloom, I could see Alfie sitting behind Radley, hanging on as if his life depended on it, and the thought of the old chap prowling through that darkened house made me smile.

'Alfie is not strong enough,' said Radley. 'We will make our way on foot. Are you with us or them, Henry?'

'I am no horseman,' said Henry, a bit too sharpish, meaning that Radley had told him what to expect. 'I would prefer to travel on foot.'

'It makes no difference to us,' said Hobbs. 'We're China bound and you may do as you please.'

'I said come on, let's be off!' One of the Irish was agitated. 'You're not the boss here, Hobbs.'

'Take our horses,' said Radley. 'You will go faster with spares.'

I heard Radley, Alfie and Henry dismount.

'Hey, posh boy,' Hobbs said threateningly. 'Your mate Dodger was not in his bed when we left. If I was to discover that you had tipped him off, I should snap your neck quick as lightning.'

'I hope China is lucky for you!' said Radley, as they kicked the horses into action.

It was not until long after the sound of hooves had fully died away and the copse was silent that Radley's shouted for me.

'Jack!'

I sprang out like a freshly oiled jack-in-the-box.

'Am I glad to see you,' I said. 'I thought you were never coming. What now?'

'We must get off the road,' said Radley. 'For sure, the search party will follow the horses' tracks. I have studied the map and we shall go across country until daybreak and then lay up. If our luck holds, they will follow the horses for a few days without realising we have gone in another direction. I hope they can navigate by the stars because, thanks to Jack, we are the only ones with a compass.' He turned to Henry. 'I must consult it to get our direction and need a few seconds of light. When I tell you, strike the flint to the tinder, let it flare a moment, then blow it out.' There was rustling as he found the map in the bag he carried over his shoulder. 'Now, Henry.' In a brief burst of yellow, I saw him peering at the compass.

'Very well,' he said. 'Follow me and pray there are not too many obstacles in our path.'

We set off into the night, the four of us holding hands like children in Hyde Park on a Sunday morning. Radley first, then Henry and Alfie, with me bringing up the rear. It weren't easy and every time one of us tripped, the rest went with him. It was funny at first and we had a good laugh until Radley stepped off the bank of a stream and plunged into the water dragging us with him. It was freezing, we all took a stomach full and, scrambling out covered in mud, weren't quite as jocular as when we started.

Henry struck the flint many times, though it was so black I couldn't tell where we were going or where we'd come from.

Radley was taking no chances and, as dawn lightened the eastern sky, decided we must stop.

'Hmm,' he said, looking hard at the map, twisting it this way and that. 'We have made progress but not as much as I hoped. We must get sleep well and make better time tomorrow.

We breakfasted on dried meat, hard bread, and a shared cup of water, before crawling under the bushes where I was asleep in minutes.

Come evening, we ate the same food, drank a little water and set off, stopping by a small brook to fill our flask and drink as much water we could hold.

As we staggered on, the new moon rose like a silver dagger and, now and then, heard dingoes and the distant bark of farm dogs, though we never saw houses nor lights.

At dawn, we crept into another bushy bed, so tired that none of us gave a fig for snakes or spiders, only for resting our weary bodies. I had no idea how far we had travelled or what the countryside looked like. Alfie's face was grey and he was breathing badly but refused help, saying he had a chill from the dousing but nothing worse.

'Jonathan,' I said. 'Tell me true. Do you know where we are?'

He chuckled. 'Let's just say I have a fair idea.' He took the compass from his pocket, laid it on the map and in the dim light pointed towards the distant hills. 'See that big one yonder? That's where we are headed. With luck, we should reach it before tomorrow morning. After that, five or six more nights and I believe we shall see the coast.'

'Then?'

'A whaler. Isn't that what you want?'

'To the United States of America?'

'I hear it is a good place for a man to start a new life,' he said. 'And we are all sorely in need of that.'

Being dog tired, I had not given food much of a thought, and by the time we set off in the morning, my guts were raging with hunger. If a search party was trying to find us all they needed to do was listen out for my belly, which was rumbling louder than thunder.

The moon grew brighter as the nights went on and we might have made better time had Alfie not been coughing badly and struggling to keep up, though he never spoke a word of complaint.

What with the rough land, it was hard going, and we were picking our way along a sloping track, when Henry stopped dead.

'Shush!'

'What?' said Radley. 'What is it?'

'Listen.'

We bent our ears, straining for the slightest sound.

'I can't hear anything save the wind,' says Radley. 'Let's be off, we cannot lose any more time.'

'No!' hissed Henry, dropping to his knees and pressing an ear to the ground. 'Take my word for it. We must leave the track now and seek cover.'

'It is only the wind, I tell you,' insisted Radley. 'What else can it be? We are in the middle of nowhere.'

'Horses,' said Henry quietly, rising to his feet. 'Believe me when I tell you I can hear horses.'

'We'll give it a few minutes,' said Radley, 'but no longer.'

Like him, I had heard nothing, and you could have knocked me down with a feather when no sooner had we climbed a little way up and crouched behind some boulders, than the sound of trotting horses burst upon our ears.

There was enough of a moon to make them out, and their riders.

Hobbs and company.

'China is not in this direction,' whispered Henry.

'I hope not,' said Radley. 'For if it is, then it is us who have been travelling in the wrong direction. No, those foolish fellows cannot steer by the stars and are lost.'

'This is bad,' I said. 'Those horses are easy to follow and now we stand between them and those who would track us down.'

'It is true,' said Alfie. 'The fools make no attempt to hide.'

'Good!' said Radley. 'While a search party is following them, they will not be following us for they think we are together. In an hour, it will be daylight. We will rest here and let them get ahead.'

We climbed higher and found our favourite beds, bushes.

'We must take turns to keep a lookout while the others sleep,' said Radley. 'You take the first watch, Jack, and Henry after you. Alfie need not take a turn.'

When the old chap protested, we told him to be quiet and get some shuteye. Over the days he had been moving slower and slower and, though it was never mentioned, we were all dreadful worried about him, especially since the cough from his days in the shed was getting worse and once again he was spitting blood from his lungs.

I found myself a good place where I could lean against a rock and peer along the track seen.

My mates were sleeping soundlessly.

The sunrise was playing tricks on my eyes, which I was having trouble keeping open an sometimes, when I stared at a bush or a tree, it turned into a man and I had to shake myself awake. To tell the truth, I must have shut my eyes for a few minutes because, before I knew it, I was looking down the track at a search party not more than a hundred yards away.

I roused the others and Radley crawled back to the rock with me.

In front, carrying a long stick and peering at the ground was the old chief from Good Hope Plantation. Some yards behind, astride a dapple mare, rode Grimshaw, a rifle laid across the saddle. After that came a squadron of twelve soldiers, formed up in pairs. It was just my luck that who should be in command but my loving sergeant from the road camp.

'They must want us back badly to send so many soldiers,' whispered Radley. 'It proves the seriousness of their crime.'

I said nothing but silently cursed Hobbs and his crew for being so stupid as to escape without knowing their way. I had to give it to Radley, he was as well prepared as any escaper could be.

A shudder went down my back when the Chief stopped right below us, holding up a hand for the others to do the same. He sniffed the air like a dog smelling fresh meat then crouched and ran his fingers through the dust.

We held our breath.

I could hear my heart beating and realised I was hanging on to Radley's shirt with whitened fingers.

'Has he found our footprints?'

'With luck Hobbs's horses will have rubbed them away,' he said. 'Pray he doesn't look too far off the track.'

Slowly, the Chief rose, scattering a handful of dry earth and watching it blow away in the breeze. He turned and, for an instant, looked directly towards where we were hiding.

'What?' shouted Grimshaw. 'What is it?'

The Chief looked away, pointed in the direction they had been riding and began running with long, loping steps.

In a minute, they had vanished.

I released my grip on Radley.

'That were a close one.'

'Too close for my liking,' he said, voice a-quiver. 'We must get out of here by another route. There is no time to waste.'

He was about to move when something else caught my eye and I pulled him down.

'Wait!'

A bush had shaken and this time it wasn't a trick of the light or my eyes deceiving me.

'Well, I'll be blowed,' said Radley.

'Me too!'

We watched in amazement as a lone figure emerged on to the track.

It was none other than Dungara who seemed to turn up everywhere like a bad penny.

Like the Chief, he sniffed the air, lowered his head and began a trot towards us. Unlike the Chief, he did not stop but passed the spot where we had left the path without glancing our way.

'He's a clever one,' I said. 'I thought I was well rid of him following me closer than a shadow. We'd best not hang around, if you ask me.'

'You're right, Jack,' he said. 'The sooner we are gone, the better.'

In a whispered conversation, we told Alfie and Henry what had happened then, after consulting the map and compass, decided on a new course. Rather than continue on the track, we would climb higher, crossing the hills on a looping route that would bring us near to Sydney and the whaling fleet at a town called Liverpool.

Alfie was not in good shape and getting worse by the hour. His skin had turned a horrible greenish colour, the sandy ground near where he had slept was spotted with blood and he was having problems rising to his feet.

I nearly cried when he said, 'Leave me lads, you'll move a deal faster without me weighing you down.'

'Nonsense,' said Radley. 'You have a bad chill from falling in the stream and will be as right as rain in a day or two.'

He laughed. 'Not I. I fear I am a goner. You'll be best leaving me, for I am the reason there are so many of them.'

'What do you mean?' asked Radley.

'Without me they cannot print their bonds and that's all that concerns them.'

'They'll find another,' Radley said.

Alfie chuckled. 'P'raps. But it changes nothing. Leave me.'

'Well, we ain't doing no such thing,' I said, angry with him for suggesting that we would even consider it. 'You've taken care of me since Portsmouth. What would I do without you to keep me in order? I should probably run wild, like them dingoes.'

It brought a smile to his face and when the others agreed with what I had said, he nodded and started as best he could up the slope.

Walking by day was easier than by night though each of us kept an eye peeled to his own point of the compass as our new route took us away from that followed by Hobbs and Grimshaw.

There was plenty of water in the brooks criss-crossing the landscape, but our store of food was almost finished. Not there had been much to start with and with all the walking we were hungrier by the step. Henry said he could trap a small animal and cook it but Radley wouldn't risk lighting a fire because the smoke would be seen for miles and, at night, the flames would give us away. We slept on empty stomachs and before setting off the following morning ate the last scraps of food, which didn't go far and served only to make me think of when we had eaten freshly baked beef pie paid for by Mr O'Connell on the Portsmouth road. As we scuffed along, I could taste the pastry melting on my tongue and the gravy trickling down my chin, until my mouth were watering like a street dog slavering over butcher's bones.

We were travelling slowly and hadn't gone hardly a mile when Alfie fell to his knees wheezing and coughing. And not for the first time.

'I say again, you must go on without me,' he said. 'I am finished, I can go no further.'

'If you cannot walk, then I shall carry you,' I said, kneeling beside him. 'You ain't a-staying here on your own, that's for sure.'

Thick blood dribbled on to his shirt. 'You would have to be double the size to put me on your back, you little blighter, but thank you all the same.'

Radley stepped up smartish.

'Henry and I will take turns. We will find a farm and leave you there, where help is at hand.'

Without more ado, he handed me his bag, stooped over, hoisted the old boy up and threw him over his shoulder as though he were a child. 'Forgive me, Alfie, I will try to be gentle and not hurt you.'

Radley was stronger than I imagined, for he kept that man on his shoulders a full two hours before his legs buckled and he was forced to let Henry take over. The pair of 'em went on like that, turn and turn about, mile after mile, with never a moan or groan. I tell you true, it's chaps like them that this world needs, not the likes of Fagin or Sikes, or McIntyre and Grimshaw, or those West End fops and their ladies going in and out of posh clubs in their fancy clothes, who would step over a starving child rather than throw 'em a crust.

I was leading the way and the sun was low in the sky when Alfie set up such a wailing that Henry had to lay him down on the grass.

'Colder than ice,' he said, placing a hand on the old boy's forehead. 'We have to get him to a place where he can rest.'

There was no shelter to be seen, nothing, not even a tree.

'Jack,' said Radley pointing up the hill we'd been climbing, 'hurry to the top and spy out what lies beyond.'

I needed no second bidding, and was off like a dog after a rabbit. Throwing myself into the long grass, I crawled the last few yards until I could peer down into a valley where a road and small river led past a farmhouse with barns and cowsheds. It was quite a spread, all neatly fenced and looking as well kept as Good Hope Plantation, but not as big.

There were horses loose in a paddock and some tethered goats nibbling at bushes, but not a person in sight. It didn't seem suspicious and I thought no more of it, being interested only in taking care of Alfie.

Next thing I knew, Radley was squirming up alongside me.

'Anything?'

'Plenty,' I said. 'We'll find food and a bed down there, that's for sure, but whether those farmers will welcome or shoot us, I shouldn't like to say.'

'I hope it is the former,' he said. 'Alfie is ill and if he is to survive, we have no choice but to find out.'

Radley and Henry supported Alfie while I went in front picking out a path clear of holes and branches that might trip them up.

By the time we reached the valley, it was dark and lantern lights were showing from inside the farmhouse, with the occasional shadow crossing a window.

Radley sent me forward alone to scout the lie of the land.

As I approached, a dog barked and I froze. Now, I ain't never had a particular love of them beasts, in fact I'm terrible a-feared of 'em, and he were a giant, tied up on the porch, snarling and leaping in my direction, the rope round its neck stopping it attacking. I scrambled behind a well when the door opened and a figure was silhouetted against the light from inside.

'What are you barking at, you horrible creature? There's nothing out there 'cept kangaroos. Shut your noise!' He aimed a kick at the dog which backed away tugging its rope, whimpering. 'And I don't want to hear any more from you, or you'll feel my stick round your ugly head!' He walked to the edge of the porch, down the steps and towards where I was hiding, a dark, powerful figure carrying a thick club that reminded me of the one wielded by Bill Sikes. He came so close, just a few feet away, that I could hear his rasping breath. There were something familiar about him though, in the dark, without seeing his face, I could not place the voice.

It seemed forever that he stood there swinging that lump of wood, before he spat in the dust, strode back to the porch and went inside, slamming the door so hard the frame rattled.

I breathed easy, but I had to find out how many more like him were in the house.

They say dogs have a good sense for who's a friend and who's an enemy. I ain't never been a dog lover, but that brute made no sound as I edged out of the shadows towards the house, scared in my guts that he'd start barking. When I was within arm's length, he sniffed, gave low growl and lay down with his head between his paws.

I knew he weren't going to go for me.

'Good boy,' I whispered, reaching out, trembling, stroking a paw the size of a man's fist. 'Stay quiet, now, I ain't going to hurt you. And you ain't going to give me away, are you?'

He gave a whimper, which I took for *no,* and I crept on towards the nearest window.

There were no curtains, and from where I was kneeling, peeking over the sill, I couldn't see much save for a woman in a rocking chair by the fire with a child asleep in her lap. On the other side I could just make out a man's legs stretched towards the flames, who I took to be the fellow who'd been on the porch.

With no other way to see inside, I crawled back towards the dog, who snuffled and licked my hand with a lolloping tongue. It weren't exactly the brightest thing to do, but having spent time in chains myself, I'm not one for seeing anything, man nor beast, tied up I unbuckled his collar and laid it on the floor at which he showed his thanks by slobbering over my face. For a moment, I felt his teeth and I wouldn't have wanted them hanging on to my leg, I can tell you.

I went once round the house, found the door to the barn, slipped the latch and went inside with the dog following like he'd been my pet since he was a puppy.

It was black as a cave at midnight, with just enough moonlight coming through the windows to see that it was stacked with straw bales. My heart pounded when I heard rustling and thought it was rats until a hen clucked as she settled back on her roost.

Outside again, I snooped a while longer but there was nothing to see.

In minutes, I was back with my mates, Henry jumping out of his skin at the sight of the hound.

'He looks like a man-eater,' he said nervously as the dog licked his hand. 'Are you sure he's not dangerous?'

Radley weren't certain, either. 'It was a bad move, bringing him, Jack. He's sure to be missed.'

Perhaps he was right, but somehow that huge, strong, friendly animal was making me feel safer.

'There don't seem to be no one around 'ceptin' for a man and a woman,' I reported. 'The barn looks the best bet to me.'

'What about workers?' asked Henry. 'This place is too big for a man and woman to manage alone. Did you see a bunk house?'

'There's no barracks, like at Good Hope,' I said. 'A cottage, a barn and a couple of sheds , that's all. I went in and there ain't no one there, I promise.'

'Then they're all in the house,' said Radley. 'There's no other explanation, which is curious, since master and men seldom sleep under the same roof.' When no one had anything to add, he said. 'Then, there's nothing for it, but to pray that all is well.'

We entered the barn, which wasn't the Savoy but was a sight more comfortable than the hillside we would otherwise have spent the night on, and made a wall of bales to hide us should anyone come in.

Alfie was shaking like a tree in a storm when we laid him down and covered him with straw to warm him up.

I had imagined that Henry had no other talent than as a carpenter, until he disappeared and returned saying he had found food and soon we would be eating a supper fit for kings. To start with, there were eggs from the chickens.

'I shall have mine fried,' I told him, 'with six slices of bacon, a lump of black pudding, and a slab of bread and butter as thick as a doorstep.'

'You will never make a gentleman,' said Radley. 'If you please, Henry, I prefer mine boiled, soft and runny, with a steaming cup of coffee.'

'Soft and runny they will be, for you'll both be eating 'em raw,' he laughed, 'and it won't do you no harm neither. Just crack 'em open and swig 'em down straight from the shell. If you ain't keen, don't worry it won't even touch the sides. There's apples for dessert, fine smelling and as crunchy as if they'd been picked this very afternoon.'

Henry, it turned out, had been brought up on a farm. He knew where chickens laid eggs, and that fruit would be stored in the attic where the air kept it cool and fresh.

'There's potatoes up there and turnips, too,' he said, 'but we daren't cook 'em into a stew, more's the pity.'

Radley took the top from the water flask, which acted as a cup, mixed two warm eggs, and fed them to Alfie who took the lot.

Then it was heads down with the hound, we had named Beast, laying next to Alfie, the heat of his body keeping the old boy warm.

Chapter 17: Friends Reunited

When I woke, the sun was streaming in, flooding the barn with light, and Hobbs was standing over me with a pitchfork aimed at my throat, ready to spike me if I made a move.

He chuckled nastily. 'Well, Dodger me lad, so you didn't get away before I'd paid you back for peaching. Now we'll see how loud you squeak while I'm striping your back, before...' he drew a finger across his throat, '...I slit your gizzard from ear to ear.'

'I know you think I turned you in,' I said feebly, 'but I had nothing to do with it, believe me, Hobbs. It was someone else.'

He took no notice. 'I knew you and Posh Boy were up to something. I could smell it.'

With that, he kicked the feet of Radley and Henry waking them from their deep sleep with a start.

'What the devil?'

'What's going on?'

The pair of them looked as if they'd seen a ghost.

'Now, now, be good boys and don't try anything funny,' said Hobbs, brandishing the pitchfork, 'or by the time I've finished with this young scoundrel you'll be able to strain cabbage though 'im.'

'Hello, hello, hello!' says another voice I now recognised from the night before. It was No Nose arriving at the run. 'Well, I'll be blowed!'

'I've caught myself a gang of trespassers,' said Hobbs. 'It's a bad business trespassing, illegal, a man could get himself hanged if he was caught. Wake the old feller up.'

'Leave him alone, he's sick,' said Henry.

'They're searching for you,' said Radley. 'We saw them. You'd best run for it before Grimshaw and his soldiers get here.'

'I took a leaf out of your book,' said Hobbs, 'and sent the Irish off with the horses. The same way you tricked us. Grimshaw'll be hot on their tail while we're at the coast boarding the first ship to who knows where. First we have to dispose of you.'

No Nose was frightened. 'We daren't kill 'em, Hobbs,' he said. 'Escaping's one thing, but murder…'

Hobbs gave him a black look. 'On yer feet, the lot of you.'

What puzzled me was where the Beast had disappeared to. There was no sign of him and he hadn't so much as barked.

We were soon to find out as they herded us to the house and there he was, on his side, panting white foam bubbling around his mouth.

When I tried to run to him, Hobbs booted the feet out from under me. 'Leave him, Dodger, or you'll be drinking a bellyful of the same.'

'What have you done, you devil,' I shouted, climbing to my feet.

'I found his collar loose on the porch. Unbuckled. Now, a doggie with them paws can't do that hisself. So, I thought, hello someone must have undone it for him. I tempted him back with a lovely piece of raw meat all dressed up with a delicious sauce made from the farmer's rat poison. I don't expect he'll last but a couple of hours.'

With Hobbs and No Nose behind, Radley and Henry supporting Alfie who was barely able to walk, we were shoved into the room I'd spied out the night before.

The farmer's wife was there, still holding her child who was snivelling, while her husband was tied to a chair. Six farm workers sat on the floor, hands and feet tightly bound.

Willis and Springer were at the stove.

Hobbs laughed. 'I found these instead of eggs.'

The pair were flabbergasted and angry.

Springer said, 'As if we ain't got enough trouble what with you takin' us 'undreds of miles in the wrong direction, and a search party on our tail. Now you have to go and find them.'

'Tie 'em up with the others and let's take the horses and get out while we've got a head start,' said Willis who was hopping mad.

'They're right,' said No Nose, 'we're wasting time.'

'We'll leave when I say so,' said Hobbs, shoving me in the shoulder so that I tumbled across the room. 'Put the old one down over there,' he ordered Radley, 'and you, No Nose, tie these three up.'

Hobbs apart, they were more interested in eating their grub than dealing with us and, as Willis roped me up, I jostled him, going through his pockets to see what I could lift. I hadn't lost my touch and he never felt a thing.

We had eaten all the eggs the night before, but it never stopped that bunch of criminals frying up pans of bacon and sausages from the pantry, which they scoffed with bread and butter. The delicious smell filling the room nearly drove us mad and it weren't long before they were ignoring us. Slowly, I let the jack-knife I'd lifted from Willis slip down my sleeve into my hand. It was hard going, but I eased the blade out of the handle and began sawing away at the rope tying my wrists. They were making so much noise chomping on their grub, that when it parted with a twang they never heard a thing. Hands free, I shifted tight up to Radley and did the same for him. He looked startled when he felt the blade but caught on in no time. Mind you, I had no plan and was hoping that he might have something in mind.

I didn't have to wait long and was as startled as those villains when he grabbed the knife, sprang to his feet and had it at Hobbs's throat, making him splutter a well-chewed mouthful of sausage across his mates before he could utter a word.

Willis and Springer were on their feet.

'Leave him be!' Hobbs shouted, trembling at the cold steel rubbing on his windpipe.

They stood off.

Then the farmer shouted, 'There's a loaded shot gun above the fireplace!'

I was across the kitchen like a greyhound, jumping on a chair and pulling the gun from its mounting. Radley pushed Hobbs away, snatched it from me and handed me the knife.

'Don't move, any of you,' he warned. 'I've shot a lot of game in my time and I don't miss. Jack, cut everyone free.'

I had their ropes off in a flash.

'Thank you,' said the farmer, rubbing the red marks on his wrists. 'You have saved our lives, for these devils would not have hesitated to kill us to cover their escape.'

The other workers had the terrible four trussed up like chickens ready for the oven, and weren't too gentle about the way they did it neither.

The farmer, John Flatley, and his wife Jane, never stopped thanking us for freeing them even though, in their hearts, they knew that we were escapers. When Alfie started coughing blood, that good woman put her child aside and knelt to soothe him.

'I think you had best eat something,' said John Flatley. 'I will pack a bag of food. Then you must be on your way, for sure as day follows night those who pursue you will be here soon enough.'

'This man cannot go with you,' said Jane, feeling Alfie's brow. 'He is too sick to travel and it will kill him if he tries.'

'We cannot leave him here,' I said. 'If'n they take him back it'll be a sight worse than dying on them hills.'

'Look at the blood, Jack,' said Radley, nodding towards Jane who was holding a reddened cloth at Alfie's mouth. 'He has no strength.'

John Flatley signalled that we should follow him and led us out of the earshot of Hobbs and his mates.

'We can hide him, and will be happy to do so. As long as those devils think he left with you when they are questioned, the trackers will believe them, and we shall confirm their story. They will have no reason to search. Rest easy. We shall take good care of him.'

'Thank you,' I said, 'he has been a father to me.'

Farmer Flatley looked sad. 'My father was transported for ten years and worked like a mule until it almost killed him. Upon his release he found a piece of land and farmed it into what I have today. One day, when our child is older, I shall go to Sydney and enter politics to fight this evil punishment.'

Radley said, 'I hope you do, for there is no justice in it.'

The farmer had a tear in his eye as he patted our shoulders and said, 'You must make haste. My workers will keep these men captive until those who seek them arrive.'

I had another task in mind. 'The Beast,' I said. 'We have to do something lest he dies.'

'What beast?' says Farmer Flatley. 'Do I need my gun?'

'Your dog, the Beast...'

'Ah, you mean Angel, she who has the temperament of those Heavenly beings.'

'...well she has been dosed with rat poison,' I said, feeling more than a little ridiculous, 'and we must attend him afore he dies.'

Farmer Flatley understood animals and knew exactly what to do. He brought a bucket of soapy water and a funnel, and while I held Angel's head, he filled the poor blighter with that horrible stuff, all of which the poor doggie vomited back as soon as his guts were full. That was the point, of course. Disgusting it was, we did it four times over until there weren't a drop of anything left inside, then carried her back to the house, laid her on the porch and covered her with a blanket.

With that doggie's vomit all over me I was stinking worse than a cess-pit until Mrs Flatley made me take a bath, albeit freezing cold, and took my togs away for washing, after which I hadn't smelled so sweet for years and the boys pretended they didn't recognise me.

We ate heartily and when the time came, carrying a bulging sack of food and with Alfie supported between Radley and Henry, we made a fine pantomime of leaving the house for the benefit of Hobbs and company.

Out of sight, we snuck the old boy into the barn, right up to the top, where there was a small loft in which he could be comfortable until danger had passed.

'Good luck, boys,' he said, 'and do not fear for me. It seems that this good man and his wife are preparing me for a life of luxury. Make all speed, and God go with you.'

'From now on he will live here,' said John Flatley. 'It is the least we can do and we will enjoy having him. Our child will have a grandparent.'

With a last handshake and a great deal of blubbing I turned to leave.

'Jack,' said Alfie, motioning me back a bit secretive.

'I must go.'

'Take these and do what you will with them.' He reached into his shirt and withdrew a package wrapped in inky cloth.

'What is it?'

'The plates I engraved for McIntyre,' he said. 'These are the reason he is pursuing us with such vigour. He has not printed from them yet and they are worth a fortune. Hide them.' I stuffed them into my shirt. 'Now, go. I will pray for your safe escape.'

There was no question that the going was a sight quicker without Alfie but, oh, how we missed that dear old chap. He was a brave soul without whom I might not have survived, and I said a little prayer that our paths would one day cross again.

Chapter 18: The Coast

The three of us lay side by side on a headland, peering across the bay to where men were moving on the decks of two whalers flying, one flying the Union Jack, the other the Yankee flag.

'I had thought we might be able to swim out,' said Henry, 'but at such a distance we shall need a boat.'

'Just as well,' I said, 'for when it comes to water I sink faster than a stone.'

'It will not be easy,' said Radley, 'and means going to the waterfront where we would be noticed in a minute. They are searching for us and in I shouldn't be surprised if our portraits aren't already gracing wanted posters in every town and village. And there'll be many ready to claim the reward.'

'There might be another way,' said Henry. 'We saw boats along the river, moored at big houses. Taking one would not be difficult. There are no soldiers or police and we could drift to the bay after dark. All the ships at anchor show lights at night so as to be seen by other craft.'

'Good thought,' said Radley. 'What say you, Jack?'

'The sooner the better,' I said. 'Let's get going.'

We were careful not to show ourselves and gave the small town, we had not learned its name, a wide berth, travelling off the roads and beyond the sight of houses, coming to the river whose course we had followed since leaving the farm.

Henry was right, every house had a small boat tied to a jetty.

'Let's do it now,' I said, 'while there's not a soul about.'

Radley shook his head. 'I think we should wait a day and see the lie of the land.'

I was itching to be off, but Henry agreed with him and that was the end of that. Besides, I had come to know that those good chaps made excellent decisions, unlike me, who was ruled by his heart not his head.

'If we keep watch tonight and tomorrow, we shall have a good idea of what to expect.'

'What if the whalers have gone,' I said panicking, for I already had a vision of myself stepping ashore in the United States of America as a free man. Not that I had any idea what Yankeeland looked like. 'What if they sail without us?'

'It is a chance we must take,' said Radley, 'and if she leaves, others will come and we shall try again.'

He slapped me hard on the back. 'Fear not, Jack, we shall make it don't you worry, though I expect we shall have an adventure or two afore we see the back of these desperate shores.'

As is often the case, his words were not far from the truth.

There ain't much to tell of that night and the following day, which were mostly boredom as two slept while the other watched the comings and goings.

It felt like a dozen or more years had passed since I'd spied out posh houses for Sikes. He'd taught me what to look for, the telltale signs you might say. One house in particular attracted us. Built of white painted wood, it sat on a bank with a boathouse of the same style in which bobbed two freshly painted skiffs[17]. Perfect for what we wanted. The trouble was, the house was busy all day long. Henry had the notion that a doctor might live there since many of the visitors had bandaged heads, arms in slings or walked on crutches. Not that it mattered. As I'd learned from Fagin, stealing is stealing whoever you pinch from. The trick is not to get caught. I did, of course, but you already know that story.

'They will not use the boats at night,' said Radley. 'Come dark, we shall make our move. Two hours drifting with the current should see us well into the bay. Then it will be a hard pull to reach that whaler. Have you ever rowed, Jack?'

---

[17] Small boat with oars and a small sail

'Hardly,' I said, 'there ain't much call for it down Piccadilly or the Strand.'

The sun dropped from sight and the few people who had been outside disappeared to their dinner tables. I was keen to be off but Radley had a cooler head and kept us waiting an hour or more before leading the way downhill and along the bank towards the boathouse.

'That one will serve our needs,' he said, pointing to the shorter of the pair. 'There are oars resting against the wall, get them, Jack.'

I was taking them down when I happened to glance out through the rear door. Coming down the path was a flickering torch, held high, flames whooshing in the breeze.

'Ssh! Hide! Someone's coming!' My stomach was turning over. We hadn't given a thought to a watchman, nor had we seen one the previous night.

Radley and Henry pressed themselves into corners, while I dived into the skiff, pulled the canvas cover over me and, all of a tremble, held my breath as the sound of boots crunching on gravel grew nearer.

I lifted a corner and peeped out through the slit.

A figure stood in the doorway, legs apart, torch held high, its light sweeping across the ceiling, his face in deep shadow.

My guts roiled at the sight of him.

He sniffed, spat and there was a plop in the water next to the boat. His free hand reached into his belt and withdrew a pistol as he made his way along the planking until I could see nothing through the crack in the canvas except the shiny toecap of his left boot inches from my face.

I was trembling, making the boat rock slightly, and had held my breath for so long that when I let it go it burst out so loud they might have heard it in the house.

Before I knew it, he had kicked off the cover and whacked me over the brain box with the pistol.

'Out, you devil. Come on, let's be having you!' he roared.

I was shaking like a jelly at the sight of Grimshaw bellowing down at me, gun pointing at my face.

'Out, I said! And quick about it afore I let you have a bullet in your criminal belly as the law entitles me.'

The mouth of the pistol followed me as I climbed out and he lowered the torch to see me better.

'Well, well, well. Thought you'd got away with it did you? Australia's a hard place to escape from and me, even harder. Where are your mates?'

'I'm alone,' I said, head swimming, voice barely a squeak. 'I got lost a few days ago. I haven't a clue where Hobbs and his lot might be.'

He pressed the gun to my head.

'I shouldn't worry about them, they're safely on their way back to Good Hope and the pleasure of

Mr McIntyre's company, so they won't know that I've gone and blown your brains out, will they? But before I do, I want them printing plates? Hand 'em over.'

I shrugged. 'Printing plates? I know nothing of such things.'

'You're Watchit's mate, where is he? And don't lie.' He pushed the gun against my forehead.

If he searched me he was going to have the surprise of his life. I was a regular little treasure trove, what with the missing printing plates and *Oliver Twist* stuck down my trousers. What a story he'd have to tell when he got back to Good Hope.

He thumbed back the hammer on the pistol. I closed my eyes and prepared for the worst.

'This is the last time I'll ask…'

'Leave him be,' said Radley from the darkness.

'No need to hurt the boy,' said Henry. 'He can't harm you.'

When I opened my eyes I could see them stepping into the light.

'And the other one?' said Grimshaw.

'Other one?' Radley sounded as innocent as a newborn lamb.

'The forger, Watchit, he's with you. That's what Hobbs told us after his tongue had been loosened with a few stripes of the whip. The four of you took off together.'

My heart jumped with joy and I knew the others felt the same. Farmer Flatley and his wife had kept Alfie safe.

'Dead!' I said, forcing out a tear. 'As dead as a doornail after all those beatings from you.'

'Do you think I believe you? He was at the farm. Where is he? Spit it out, you cheeky young...' Grimshaw was about to whack me across the head, when he changed his mind and laughed. 'You'll pay for that lie with a hundred extra kisses from the cat when I get you back to...'

He never finished the sentence. A figure had stepped out of the shadows and struck him on the head with a length of wood.

As Grimshaw fell, Radley caught up the torch and turned it on the new arrival.

Radley did not know him, nor Henry, but I stared in astonishment. I did.

'Good evening,' he said softly then, with a slight chuckle in his voice, 'It seems I made a first class job of your feet, young fellow. They have healed well for you to travel such a distance on foot.'

'Surgeon Holmes!' I could barely get out his name. I could not have been more surprised if Queen Victoria herself had appeared and pardoned us on the spot.

'This is my house,' he said, 'and I believe you were about to steal my boat.'

'I am sorry,' I said, pathetically. 'We had no other choice.'

'Is that so? There are many boats on the river, but you chose mine.'

'More like it chose us,' I said. 'It were just sitting here waiting.'

'I suppose you are making for the bay, hoping to find an American whaler. That's what most escapers try. Few make it, of course. But you might just be in luck. There are two at anchor this very night, the Cormorant is the larger vessel and British flagged, so I suggest that the Pequod will suit you better, though her Captain has a reputation as something of a demon. Her berth is nearest to the river mouth, and she sails on the midnight tide for Japan.'

I couldn't believe what I was hearing, and nor could the others whose mouths were gaping as wide as fish on the counter at Billingsgate Market.

'You're going to let us go?' whispered Henry, eyes on stalks in disbelief.

'Transportation and harsh punishment for minor crimes may be the law of England, but personally I detest it. It is inhuman and achieves nothing except misery for the families of those poor souls sent here,' he said. 'I am acquainted with Mr McIntyre of Good Hope Plantation and stay there when I am in that part of the country. His men are staying here while they search for you but, in all conscience, I cannot let them take you back for I know the punishment you will receive.' He sighed. 'Take the boat and go now, quickly, before he wakes.'

I said, 'He'll know it was you what flattened him. You'll be in deep trouble yourself.'

Surgeon Holmes shook his head. 'I heard what he said. He didn't see me and will think it was the missing fourth man who hit him. I will help convince him it was so. Mark you, he will know where you have gone and will follow. I will not be able to stop him. I beg you, waste no more time.'

With that I shook that good man's hand and so did Radley and Henry. We dived into the skiff and when we pulled into the river he was nowhere to be seen, only Grimshaw unconscious on the planks the torch flickering beside him.

The current was strong, the night sky clear and the river flooded with moonlight as we were swept towards the sea, keeping well away from the banks. I have no idea how long it took because my head was spinning with excitement.

After a while, Radley said, 'What did Grimshaw mean when he asked about the printing plates?'

'Alfie gave 'em to me,' I said, tapping the bulge in my shirt. 'We are to do what we want with 'em.'

'In the right hands they are worth a great deal of money,' he said.

'How much?' asked Henry.

'Imagine more money than you can spend in ten lifetimes,' he said. 'Imagine living like a lord.'

'A small house, and food on the table would suit me,' answered Henry. 'What about you, Jack?'

'I should change my name to Lord Buffington,' I said. 'Buy a new suit, a horse and carriage and live in a posh hotels in Mayfair. And no more gin and oysters[18], only the finest beef and port wine at every meal.'

---

[18] What are now luxuries were common food at the time

There weren't time to continue, for we had just cleared a low headland and the water suddenly grew rougher making us bend harder to the oars.

'There!' shouted Radley. 'Pull for that light. That's the Pequod, I hope.'

We went at it like demons, arms hauling on the oars until our backs ached and I feared my shoulders would part from my body.

The first we knew that all wasn't right was when we heard a loud crack and something whizzed between me Henry like a bumble bee looking for a fight.

'It must be Grimshaw,' called Radley. He had turned around and was searching the night. 'I see them! And they're firing at us.'

True enough. The sea was sparkling in the moonlight and silhouetted against it was a boat with a man standing in the bow. Faintly, his voice came to us across the water.

'Pull you men! Pull hard! There's a golden guinea for every one of you when those devils are taken.'

Grimshaw! The man would not go away.

Another shot, and this time it blew a large splinter out of the bow, which flew up taking a chunk out of my cheek just below the eye. I'm carrying the mark to this day, and proud of it.

When I tasted blood trickling into my mouth, it made me pull doubly hard. Henry too, for it splattered his face and, for a moment, he thought it was his.

Truth is, when it came to rowing, we were no match for them. They were gaining fast and bullets were beginning to make their mark. Whoever was firing was a top marksman considering it was night and the boats were bobbing like corks.

Then they hit Radley. There was a crack, he pitched forward and I feared he were dead.

He wasn't.

'Pull you weaklings! Pull!' he cried, writhing in the bottom of the boat. 'We'll make it if those Yankees'll let us aboard.'

Me and Henry were pulling with our backs to the whaler and never knew how close we were, only that we could see Grimshaw's villains gaining on us with every stroke.

For the first time I heard shouting.

'Come on boys, stretch those arms.'

'Heave ho, English fairies. Put your backs into it.' They were speaking our language alright, but with a twang I'd never heard the likes of, calling us on, encouraging us to go faster.

Yankees!

The marksman cracked off another shot that took a lump out of Henry's oar next to his hand.

'Lord love us!' he gasped. 'That was too close for my liking.'

We were pretty nigh done, worn out from heaving those heavy oars. Grimshaw's boat was gaining fast, as if they were running and we were walking, and that devil was standing in the bow swinging a grappling hook on the end of a rope.

It was then I spotted Dungara sitting behind Grimshaw, eyes fixed on me. He had led them to us. After what he had been through, who was I to blame him.

When Grimshaw let go of the rope it looped high in the air and dropped into our boat, the spikes had dug in, catching on the stern, and he had yanked tight. We had been hooked like fish and he was hauling us in, laughing like a maniac.

'Got the lot of you! I'll have the hide off your scurvy backs, just you wait. Especially you, Artful Dodger. Yes, I know who you are!'

He knew my nickname and must have learned it from Hobbs and company. Not that it made any difference, the cat was going to sting and cut my flesh just the same, whatever name I was going by.

Roped up, they closed the distance between us in no time, and no matter how hard we rowed, we were getting nowhere.

Radley had managed to sit up upright and was preparing to fight Grimshaw who was readying himself to jump the gap between the boats. He was brandishing a wooden club and I could almost feel it battering my skull.

The Yankee crew was still urging us on and I could tell that their voices were nearer.

Grimshaw leapt.

The boats crashed together, their bow running up over our stern.

Radley grabbed Grimshaw's legs only to receive a blow to the skull. A second man was preparing to board when there was an almighty thud and we stopped dead, Henry and me being flung from our seats.

All four of us were sprawling in the boat when something heavy fell over us.

'Climb you Limey[19] landlubbers, climb,' a voice was shouting from above. 'Climb!'

We had smashed into the side of the whaler, and the crew had thrown down a clambering net.

'Climb! Come on, boys. You must do it yourself for if we help we shall be in trouble with your government who will arrest our ship. Once on board you will be safe. Climb you Limey fairies, climb!'

Henry threw himself on Grimshaw, kicking and punching while I dragged Radley from beneath him.

'Up the net,' I told him, noticing for the first time his blood soaked shirt where a lead ball had gone clean through his shoulder.

'I cannot do it, Jack,' he said. 'I cannot use my right arm.'

I knew what he would have told me had it been the other way round, so I said, 'Then use your left, you lazy man. That blighter's working properly ain't it?'

He set to as I leapt upon Grimshaw. Another of his men jumped aboard our craft, which was rocking alarmingly what with all the action. He

---

[19] The American name for English sailors who were given lime juice to prevent scurvy

was a big chap and landed uneasily setting us rolling from side to side so that water rushed in.

The boat was going down fast as we toppled into the water. Henry and I let go of Grimshaw and I began sinking like a stone. You see, you don't learn to swim working the streets of London, and a dip in the filthy Thames was as sure a death sentence as hanging at Newgate.

If it were black above the waves, it were a sight blacker below and a good deal wetter. How far I sank I have no idea, but my lungs were bursting by the time I started rising to the surface.

When I broke through, I was a long stretch off the whaler. Our boat had disappeared and there were men in the water all around, shouting for help, but no sight of Henry. I thrashed around, trying to swim but to no avail and in seconds I was on my way down again, heading for what Jack Tars call Davy Jones's Locker.

It's a dangerous place the ocean, and why any man would want to spend his life on it ha dalways been a mystery to me.

When I came up I could see the whaler a hundred feet away. A light hung on the stern and I could see the name, Pequod. Radley was hauling himself up using one arm, and Henry was not far behind. Then I felt a hand on my shoulder and swung my head round to be confronted by none other than Grimshaw, hair plastered across his face, grinning like a shark that's just caught itself a fat dinner.

He grabbed for my collar, missed and punched me in the face, making my head swim. Then he had me by the throat and was raining blows down on my head.

I was no match for him until I felt those metal plates in my shirt and used 'em to wallop him across the brain box. Then he let go quick enough.

Not that it did me much good, and I went down a third time. I have heard it said since, that a drowning man's life flashes before him. I'd often wondered how they knew, what with him being dead and all, but I'm here to tell you it's true. At that moment, I weren't afraid of dying and, as I sank, my lungs filling with water, everyone I ever knew was standing before me; Oliver on the road to London, Bill Sikes and Nancy, my mate Charley and the gang, the magistrate, the Peeler, Hobbs's lot, Surgeon Holmes, the Sergeant, McIntyre and Grimshaw, Farmer Flatley and Jane. Fagin was swinging in the breeze, coat billowing out like a ship under sail, but he weren't dead, he were smiling and waving at me as if I was to go with him. The whole lot of 'em, villains included, looking like angels and waiting for me to join 'em.

I was staring at a pair of boots, coughing and spewing seawater from my mouth and nose. Someone was holding me upside down by the ankles and shaking hard. Once or twice my head whacked whatever was underneath, though it didn't hurt much. It weren't exactly medical treatment such as a rich gent might have received in St Bart's, but it was doing the trick. I was alive and breathing.

'He's empty,' I heard as I was dropped roughly on my face. 'He swallowed half the harbour!'

How I'd survived I hadn't a clue, but I had. Now, I was captured again and it would be the worse for me. I just hoped that Radley and Henry had managed to climb aboard the Pequod.

'Tell me your name,' said the same voice.

'You know it well enough,' I gurgled.

'Are we acquainted?' says he. 'I cannot remember ever setting eyes upon your ugly face. Then, I am getting on in years and my old Yankee eyes do not always give me good service.'

Yankee eyes?

I looked up from the deck.

It weren't Grimshaw nor any of his cronies.

He was staring down, a giant leg planted either side of my body. I say that, though one weren't a leg at all but a wooden post from the knee down. He was a bear of a man dressed in white trousers, brass-buttoned coat and a strange hat, like a misshapen topper, the likes of which I'd never seen. He was bearded but without a moustache and there was something of the religious about him that reminded me of the mad preacher we used to taunt on the steps of St Paul's Cathedral. There was quite a gang behind him including Henry who had a smile on his face as wide as the Pacific Ocean.

'Jack Dawkins, sir,' I said, by way of introduction. 'May I be so bold as to ask yours?'

'I am Captain Ahab,' he said, gruffly. 'Master of this vessel, the Pequod, which you have boarded uninvited.'

'Where is Radley?'

'Your other friend is below decks, being stitched up,' said the Captain.

'He wouldn't have made it but for you, Jack,' chipped in Henry.

'Seems I'm lucky to be here,' I said. 'All I remember is someone shouting that we had to get on board without help. One minute I'm drowning then, next, here I am surrounded by angels. Give us a kick, Henry, just to prove I'm not a goner.'

Henry did. A light tap that didn't hurt a bit and even if it had I wouldn't have cared.

'How did I do it?' I asked. 'My life was flashing in front of me.'

'You've him to thank,' said Captain Ahab, shoving a brown chap into my view.

'Dungara!'

'He swam you to the ship,' said Henry, 'and dragged you up the net single-handed. How he did it, I don't know. For a little 'un, he has the strength and determination of an ox.'

It was a shock, I can tell you. I looked that aborigine direct in the eye. 'Why?' I said. 'Why did you save me?'

He never said a blinkin' word, just looked back at me as if I was a brick wall in an Eastcheap alley.

I didn't know what to say and turned back to Captain Ahab. 'Won't you be arrested by the authorities for taking us on board?'

'It was not my choice to have you on the Pequod,' he said, 'but my crew are a soft-hearted bunch and sought to save you. There are some British amongst them with every reason to dislike your Queen's government. We were readying for sea when you and your pursuers came alongside. I am pleased to say that your British laws do not prevent us from saving drowning men. I hope these shores will be many days behind us before you confess who you are.' He held up a warning hand to prevent me answering. 'I would rather not hear it now and would be obliged if you will hold your tongue and say nothing to implicate this ship in whatever reason your pursuers had for capturing you. By which time it will be too late.'

'We will work for our keep,' said Henry, ready to please the man who had saved our lives.

'Oh, be sure you will,' he roared. 'Life on a whaler is tough and there'll be no pay but grub a-plenty. As soon as the doctor has seen the young 'un and made sure he'll live, the cook will rustle you up some food and you can get some shut eye. Tomorrow you'll be scrubbing decks.'

With that he turned his back and stumped off, wooden leg banging the deck. It was be impossible to mistake Captain Ahab's footfall.

Chapter 19: Leaving Australia

It was another week before the three of us felt truly safe and free again as Pequod sailed up the east coast of Australia on a heading for Japan. Dungara kept himself to himself and every time I approached him to offer thanks for saving my life, which was pretty well whenever I saw him, he ran away.

I heard Captain Ahab a long way off. Clunk – clunk – clunk. When it stopped, he was standing there looking more ferocious than ever.

'Good morning, Captain.'

'That is not the Bible you are reading,' he said.

'It is called Oliver Twist, sir,' I replied, 'by the great author Charles Dickens.'

'I have never heard of the man,' he said. 'I read only the Good Book which is enough for any God-fearing man.'

I saw a curious glint in his eye just then. We were to spend many months aboard the Pequod and it was something I was to see many times and which would come back to haunt my dreams, turning them into nightmares.

'Who taught you reading? It is unusual for a person of your class. There are few in my crew, who are able to understand words.'

'A fine man called Alfie Watchit,' I said, 'on the prison ship from Portsmouth to New South Wales. We had a Bible. I read it a lot. He took care of me like the father I never had. We escaped together, the four of us.'

'And this Watchit fellow, was he killed by your pursuers?'

'I believe he is safe on a farm where he will live out the rest of his days in comfort,' I told him.

'And that one,' he nodded at Dungara crouching on the deck, staring in that way of his. 'What is his interest in you?'

'To be honest, sir,' I said, 'I do not know, but I believe he thinks that I wronged him.'

'He saved your life. Perhaps it was to revenge himself later. Did you play him foul?'

I looked the Captain straight in the eye. 'I did not, sir. Though I might have prevented him taking a flogging if I had spoken up.'

'And you did not?'

'I had been flogged myself aboard the vessel carrying us to Australia. Had I said anything, it would have meant another taste for me. I could not stomach it.'

'You speak honestly, at least,' he said. 'Show me the book.'

I handed it to him.

'It has taken something of a battering.' He turned it over, riffling the pages now curled from seawater.

'It took a swim with me,' I said..

'I do not approve of such works,' he said, 'but at least you are able to read, which is a sight more than most.' He handed it back. 'Find yourself a Bible and learn the words by heart. It will do you more good than that rubbish.'

'I will try, sir,' I said, wishing to keep on his good side.

'Then get back to your work. You're paying for freedom, remember.'

'Aye-aye, sir,' I said in the manner of my shipmates when they spoke to a superior.

He stumped off a few paces, stopped as if thinking and turned back.

'You would do well to befriend that black boy.'

'Yes, sir,' I said. 'I shall try.'

At first, I imagined that he had lost the leg in some great naval battle, but it weren't entirely true. There had been a battle by all accounts, and a right royal affair too, but with a harpooned whale, which was so strong it had upturned the Captain's longboat and bitten off his leg at the knee.

Imagine that, coming face to face in the ocean with a whale, and him taking a lump out of you. You'd have nightmares for the rest of your days.

Since that time, the crew said, Captain Ahab's every waking moment had been dedicated to finding that giant whale – Moby Dick, was its name – and killing it. He frightened me, I have to admit. I've sailed both great oceans, the Atlantic and the Pacific, and I know how big those beasts can be. So, ask yourself, what kind of a man is it that thinks he can find one particular whale in all that water? I've met some rum types in my time, but Captain Ahab took the biscuit.

Not that I let him, or Moby Dick, worry me. Like Radley, who's health was improving, and Henry who had become the Pequod's carpenter, I was pleased to be free, with the wind blowing me further from Australia and Queen Victoria's goalers by the hour.

I'd sailed to Australia as a convict, behind bars and under guard, and now I was sailing away, not free exactly, but without chains and hopeful of a new start in life. I wanted to leave the Artful Dodger, Fagin, Sikes and their kind behind. The same for all those rotten guards and people who called themselves ladies and gentlemen when, if the truth were told, were worse criminals than the whole thieving lot of us put together. There were good 'uns, of course, even in that place, Farmer Flatley and Surgeon Holmes being like angels in hell.

I stood up and strolled over to Dungara, stretching my hand out before me. Slowly, and to my great surprise, he rose and took it in his own. We stood there like silly statues not knowing what to do next until I found my voice.

'I'm sorry for what I did,' I told him, meaning every word of what I was saying. 'I'm ashamed and I want to make it up to you. But seeing as how you ain't got a clue what I'm talking about, you'll never know.'

He nodded in the manner of an old professor, and said in stuttering English. 'I want to be your friend.'

You could've knocked me over with a wet rag.

'You speak our language.'

'My grandfather spoke it. He made me learn. He said it was best to understand what our masters were saying.'

'You never said a word at your trial, nor peached.'

'Peached?'

'Never told 'em it was me as nicked the book. And you never told 'em where we were hiding on the road, neither, did you? You saw us. And you must have known Alfie was still at the farm.'

'I want to be friends,' he said.

'I am truly sorry,' I said, and I have to confess the way he was looking at me and asking for us to be mates, a tear weren't far off.

'We can help each other,' he said.

Letting bygones be bygones seemed to make sense, and from that day on, we did, the four of us working hard by day, squatting on the deck, talking and laughing by night.

Dungara picked up English quickly and told us about Alfie and how the old boy was safe, carefully hidden at the top of the barn by farmer Flatley. He had poked around, as was his way, and found him, but had not given him up. Afterall, he hated Grimshaw and McIntyre as much as the rest of us.

It was Radley who brought up the subject of the printing plates and we had another long discussion about how we would live like kings and have palaces next to each other on the same street. All except Dungara, who said he would prefer a nice shelter in the open air.

Funny thing was, I thought they'd be disappointed when I told them that the last time I'd seen them they were sinking in the ocean along with Grimshaw.

In fact, I think they were glad. We'd all had enough of being criminals.

Everything had changed.

I had been given another chance to make the most of what I had.

My old life was gone.

Or almost all of it.

There was only one thing left to remind me of my days as a thief in London. The book, *Oliver Twist*.

I walked to the rail and held it above the ocean, listening to the wind riffling the paper as if the characters on those pages were talking to me, saying goodbye. I closed my eyes tightly and let go.

The book fell.

They were gone.

My old life was behind me. The Artful Dodger and chums were sinking to Davy Jones' Locker.

'Jack! What are you doing?'

I opened my eyes.

It was Henry.

'You can't do that, not after all you've been through. That was your history.'

'Not any more' I said. 'Jack Dawkin's life starts now and I think, in future, I shall call myself…'

Henry laughed. 'I caught it.'

'You did what?'

'Here! I didn't think you really wanted to be rid of it.' He handed it back. 'Believe me, in years to come you would've been sorry.'

'Thank you,' I said, taking it back. 'You're a real pal, Henry.'

Over the years I've had many opportunities to dump it, but in the end could never bring myself to do the deed. And Henry was right, I would've been sorry, since Fagin and the likes turned out to be cherubs compared with some of the villains I was to meet later on.

'Storm clouds ahead!' It was the call of the lookout high in the crow's nest.

He had never uttered a truer word.

THE END

TRANSPORTATION TO AUSTRALIA FINALLY CEASED IN 1868 AFTER 80 CRUEL YEARS.

JACK DAWKINS RETURNS IN

DODGER & DICK

Aboard the whaling ship, Pequod, Jack and his companions encounter the Great White Whale, Moby Dick

15807240R00128

Printed in Great Britain
by Amazon